WATISHKA WARRIORS

WATISHKA WARRIORS

Daniel Auger

© 2008 by Eschia Books Inc.
First printed in 2008 10 9 8 7 6 5 4 3 2 1
Printed in Canada

The Publisher: Eschia Books Inc.

Library and Archives Canada Cataloguing in Publication

Auger, Daniel, 1956–
Watishka Warriors / by Daniel Auger.

ISBN 978-0-9810942-2-9

1. Indian reservations—Juvenile fiction. I. Title.
PS8601.U383W38 2009   jC813'.6   C2009-900206-X

Project Director: Kathy van Denderen
Project Editor: Pat Price
Cover Design: Joy Dirto
Cover Image: Frank Burman / Photos.com
PC: 1

To Mom
For everything…

Acknowledgements

This book would not have been possible without the support, encouragement and input from so many people. My thanks go to Pat Price, for helping shape this story from an idea into reality. To my fiancée and son for their ongoing support and love in my writing. And to all of those who give me the opportunity to tell my stories—they would not exist without you.

Prologue

he wind was so strong, it drowned out Lawrence Arcand's cries of despair.

The howl echoing across the field of moonlit snow seemed to match his sobs pitch for pitch, as if he were making no sound at all. In the noise that surrounded him, Lawrence felt silent and alone.

Just like always... he thought.

The freezing wind blew back the fur-lined hood of his parka as he slogged through the knee-deep snow. He couldn't feel his ears anymore, but he didn't care. It was only a matter of time before he didn't feel anything. He reached into the pocket of his parka and pulled out the rye he'd been drinking most of the evening. The liquor burned his mouth but did nothing to dull his unbearable pain.

You're not like us, she'd said. You're nobody.

Lawrence was more than familiar with alcohol; most people on the reserve were, some more than others. His own father was, at this very moment, passed out on the sofa at home. It hadn't been hard for Lawrence to slip the bottle of rye from his father's slack hand. He'd paused once to take in the scene one final time—the stained carpeting, the sagging furniture, the bullet holes in the living room wall, and his father, undershirt barely covering his growing paunch, snoring on the couch as the 20-year-old television blared. Lawrence wondered if he should leave a note or at least hug him, but when he touched his father's hand, he felt no warmth, no response. Instead, he'd stashed the rye in his jacket pocket, thrown open the front door and stumbled out into the cold.

As he trudged through the snow, Lawrence gave a fleeting thought to his mother, who'd left with a man from a southern reserve when Lawrence was seven. Lawrence hadn't seen her since; she'd never returned, never called, never wrote. Had she ever given a thought to him in the seven years since she'd left? *Probably not*, he thought miserably. She'd abandoned him, just like everyone else.

He wondered if anyone would miss him. His father, maybe—when he wasn't drunk. And Cody. Lawrence felt a sudden pang of guilt. He'd known Cody since they were kids. Unlike everyone else on the reserve, who seemed to take pleasure in bullying him, Cody had always treated him like a friend.

He'll be fine, Lawrence thought. *He's got other friends. Not like me.*

The only other person who seemed to understand him was Alicia. Lawrence had known her almost all his life. As kids, they'd played. As teenagers, they'd started to play around. One night, after the Posse crashed a dance at the community hall, she and Lawrence had fled into the surrounding bushes and, standing against a graffitied monument to a First Nations leader no one really remembered, they had kissed for the first time. He was in love.

As long as he had Alicia, he could almost bear his miserable life. But then everything had changed. Alicia was beautiful—and the Posse had noticed. Lawrence took another swig of rye and scowled. *This was their fault,* he thought, hatred coursing through him. They were drug dealers, thieves, bullies. They tormented everyone, robbing gas stations and dealing drugs. They were always drunk or high and drove around the reserve in beat-up cars, causing trouble. The only people they didn't terrorize were their brothers and sisters, but Lawrence didn't have either. Instead, they'd made him a target. They sped past him in their cars, sometimes throwing empty beer cans in his direction.

He knew Alicia was too good for him, but he never thought…

A whistle rose above the howling wind. It was time. He drained the bottle and tossed it aside then began to shuffle down the hill to the railroad tracks. He could see a faint speck of light a few kilometres off.

At the bottom of the hill, he stumbled then picked himself up and paused by the tracks. He felt no fear, no anxiety. No voices told him that what he was doing was wrong. All he heard was Alicia's voice.

"You're nothing, Lawrence," she'd said, as she hopped into the Posse car and wrapped herself around the tough-looking man inside.

"Nothing."

Lawrence slumped to his knees, his eyes frozen shut with tears, his spirit exhausted. Crawling forward, he felt the gravel under his shins and then cold steel as his knee contacted the rail. He fell forward onto the tracks and rolled onto his back, staring up at the stars.

"I am nothing," he whispered.

With a heavy sigh, Lawrence surrendered his spirit to the heavens.

Anne lay in bed, unable to sleep. Her hips ached, and, tonight, even the special salve she often used wasn't working. Something was wrong; she could feel it in the air.

She heard the whistle of the train—right on time, as usual—and a moment later, the screech of the wheels on the track.

Oh, no…, Anne moaned softly. *Not again!*

How many times had she heard that sound? How many more would lose their lives?

This must stop! she thought. *But how?*

She needed spiritual guidance.

Pushing back the quilts, Anne eased herself out of bed then pulled a worn blanket around her shoulders. Ignoring the complaints from her hips, she settled into an overstuffed chair in the corner. Then she closed her eyes and began murmuring quietly in Cree.

The old man stood at the top of the hill, observing the chaos in the valley below.

An RCMP vehicle's emergency lights flickered in the darkness, and men in uniforms and coveralls were talking on radios, taking measurements and hammering stakes into the frozen ground. Another man was holding out his arms, shaking them as he talked to a uniformed officer. On the tracks was a white tarp, covering something no one wanted to see.

The old man shook his head sadly. It was a scene he had witnessed far too often. It needed to stop. The time had come to act before another *oskinîkiw* decided life wasn't worth living.

Closing his eyes, the old man lifted his face to the sky. His lips began to move, as he gently whispered in his mother tongue. After a few moments he stopped and opened his eyes.

Then he gathered his blanket around him and disappeared into the bush.

Chapter One

Cody Gladue stood in his driveway, hockey stick in hand, and fired a tennis ball off the side of the wood-frame house. *Thunk, thunk, thunk.* The ball was frozen solid, but Cody didn't care.

The beauty of living in a small community was that everyone knew everyone. The bad thing was that the same fact was true, and bad news travelled fast.

Lawrence, he thought painfully, whacking his stick hard against the ball. *How could you?* Lawerence wasn't the first kid to lie down on the tracks—Cody knew that. But this time it was different. This was Lawrence, his friend.

There was a crunch of snow behind him, but Cody didn't turn. He didn't want anyone to see his tears.

"Cody." It was Nicky Fox. A tall shadow cast over his shoulder told him Stan Laboucan was there, too.

"What?" Cody answered hoarsely. He wiped his eyes with a corner of a sleeve.

"You heard?"

Cody nodded, winding up with a slapshot that crashed into the wall.

"Sucks, man," Stan said in his deep, gentle voice.

"He had nothing," Nicky said. "Dad's a bum. No older brother. What was he going to do?"

Cody wheeled around, letting the ball trickle down the driveway. "He didn't have to do that," he said, eyes flashing. Tears were streaming down his face again, but he didn't care. "He could've talked to me!"

"What could you do, Cody?" Nicky asked. "You know Lawrence didn't fit in. He was miserable, man."

"Yeah," Stan said. "You couldn't have stopped him."

"Lawrence just figured he didn't have any other choice," Nicky said solemnly, picking at a sliver of wood on his hockey stick. "And maybe he was right. What choice do any of us have?"

Cody didn't reply. It was true. No one on the reserve had much in the way of choices. They were all trapped, confined to a small number of equally crappy options—Posse, gas station, oilfields, death. The Posse recruited at 16; he, Stan and Nicky had two years before they had to face their future.

"I would have helped him," Cody said. "I would have tried to help him."

There was a momentary silence, as they stared at the frozen ground.

"We can't help him now," Nicky said finally, rapping his stick on the gravel. "C'mon. Let's play."

Sheldon Lambert was furious. And everyone could tell.

Rage Against the Machine was blasting from the stereo, and Sheldon, sprawled on his bed, was raging along, his voice rising even higher whenever a four-letter-word erupted from the speakers. The thump of the bass rattled the shelves in his room, threatening to topple his hockey trophies. Sheldon wished one would fall on his head and knock him out. Or, better still, on his coach's head.

You need to change your attitude, Coach Fernley had said.

Sheldon had let the coach know exactly what he thought about his comments, using some of the same words he was using now.

That's exactly why you're not playing for this team, the coach had replied.

Sheldon had yelled all the way off the ice, smashing his hockey stick against the boards and shouting about how they were just cutting him from the bantam AAA hockey team because people in Grande Prairie didn't like Indians. He knew it wasn't true—three other aboriginal players had survived the first round of cuts—but it was an argument Sheldon often used when he didn't get his way.

During the two-hour ride home with his father, he'd sat in the back seat of their beat-up station wagon, ignoring his father's attempts at conversation. Sheldon wasn't used to rejection. He wasn't used to being told he wasn't good enough. And he wasn't happy about having to go back home to Watishka Lake.

This was supposed to have been his break. He'd been playing hockey in Manning since he was five, and he was good—great even. One of the best players around, everyone said. His parents knew it, too—his mom had even gotten a job to help pay for his equipment and registration fees. By seven, he could skate circles around the rest of the kids in Manning, scoring 65 goals in one 25-game season. He was the best player in his league, and everyone knew it.

"You're gonna be big, bro," his brother, Lou, told him. "You're gonna make the big time, the big leagues, easy.

"And if you don't, I got your back."

An assistant coach with the bantam AAA Thunder in Grande Prairie had heard about Sheldon. He'd driven out to Manning and, after watching just one game, offered him a tryout. If he made the team, they'd find room and board for him and even put him through school.

It was supposed to keep going from there. From bantam AAA, he'd go to midget AAA and attract the attention of the WHL. He'd be a high draft choice, then make the leap to junior. From there, it was only a matter of time until he played in the World Junior Championships then get picked first overall in the NHL. He'd make the big leagues, make the big money and never, *ever* have to come back to Watishka Lake again—which was exactly what Sheldon wanted.

He hated this place, this dive, this shithole. The reserve was for losers. Okay, so maybe some of the older folks, like his Dad, had done all right, but he wasn't going to stay. Hockey was his ticket out of here. Without hockey, he only had one option. And he didn't know how he felt about that choice, no matter how much Lou pushed him.

Sheldon's tryout had lasted one weekend. His name was one of the first called. Now his dream was lying in a shattered pile of fibreglass at a rink in Grande Prairie, and he was lying in his bedroom back on the Watishka Lake reserve, swearing along with the music.

Chapter Two

andy Lafonde's body was telling her it was later than it actually was. She was definitely ready for bed.

It's always worse flying west, she thought to herself. *Or is it east?*

It wasn't as if she'd flown in from Russia. The difference in time between Alberta and the Bahamas was only two hours.

The difference in the weather, however...

Sandy grumbled inwardly, staring through the windshield at the snow and ice stretching out to the horizon. It had been a beautiful 26°C when she'd boarded the plane on the island. According to the temperature gauge in the rental SUV, it was −33°C, a temperature she hadn't had to deal with since she'd last visited Aunty Anne. *God, how long had it been? Three years?*

Sandy felt a pang of guilt. *I've been away too long.*

Sandy never really liked coming back to the reserve. It was depressing, and nothing ever seemed to change. But she missed her aunt, who had raised her since birth, when her own mother had left her with Aunty Anne and then just disappeared.

Plus, she'd had that email from Sherry.

Aunty Anne wasn't doing well, Sherry had written. Her arthritis had gotten worse, especially in her hands and hips, and she was having trouble getting around. But what was really worrying everyone was her mental state. Sherry had gone to visit one day and found Aunty Anne sitting in her rocking chair, her head drooping, murmuring to herself in Cree. At Sherry's touch, she had roused quickly, but she seemed to take a few moments to remember where she was and what she was doing. It had happened several times since then, worrying Sherry enough to write.

Of course, Sandy had come right away. Not knowing how long she would be away, she'd notified her boss that she might not be back for a few weeks. Doug had kissed her goodbye at the airport and wished her luck.

"Why don't you come with me?" she'd asked.

"You know why," Doug had replied.

Sandy did know why. But she hadn't figured out a way to solve that problem yet.

Sandy glanced at the clock. She'd forgotten how long a drive it was from Edmonton to the reserve. The sun was long gone, and night was stealing over the horizon. She spotted an intersection just ahead; the headlights dimly lit the sign reading *Watishka Lake First Nation: 10 KM.*

Flipping on her left-turn signal, she made the turn off Highway 35. The road was rutted and uneven. She flicked on her high beams and clutched the wheel, every bump emphasizing her conflicting emotions. Through the windshield, she could see a few dots of light, haphazardly scattered across hundreds of acres. A waxing moon hung in the sky, its cool, white light shining a path across the frozen, crusted snow. She shivered. Doug and the Bahamas seemed far, far away.

Half an hour later, she came to a cracked stone sign, the

only indication she was about to cross the threshold onto the reserve.

Welcome to Watishka Lake First Nation, it read. Below, half obscured by graffiti, was the same greeting in Cree.

Sandy sighed as she looked out the windows of the SUV—little had changed since she'd left the reserve 13 years ago. Houses were scattered randomly over large plots of land bisected by gravel roads. Many of the homes were in disrepair, their roofs missing shingles, the windows broken, the wood siding rotted and only half-painted. Others had no front stairs. Sandy saw, a few hundred metres ahead, a car with only one working headlight careen across the road—in reverse gear.

She drove past the gas station, with its single pump, and was surprised to see it open. The only business on the reserve, the station was sometimes open, at other times boarded up. Every time an owner closed it down, someone else snapped it up. There would be talk of more pumps, a restaurant or even a car wash, but nothing ever materialized. The gas station sign was the brightest light on the reserve, a false beacon of hope in the darkness.

Continuing up the road, she passed the community centre, one of the few reserve buildings in good repair, thanks to the elders. She wondered if Alexander Bullchild was still chief. Further along, five or six boys, hockey sticks in hand, were batting a tennis ball around under a lone streetlamp. Street hockey was popular on the reserve, but it was usually played with a little more pep, she thought, as she drove by.

Sandy spied a familiar intersection ahead. Excitement growing, she turned onto the gravel road leading up to Aunty Anne's house. She saw a car in the driveway as she pulled up. Sandy wasn't surprised. Aunty Anne was a reserve elder, and it was common for her to have company. She ran up the front steps and opened the front door.

"Hello?" Sandy dropped her bags and tossed her parka onto a hook by the door. "Aunty Anne?"

Hearing voices from the kitchen, Sandy headed in that direction, pausing for a moment to run her hand over a handmade rocking chair in the living room. Aunty Anne's grandfather had made the chair many, many years ago. It was worn smooth from use but still sturdy. Though newer, more comfortable furnishings had made their way into the room, the chair remained Aunty Anne's favourite. Eventually, Sandy realized, it would come to her.

She hesitated at the kitchen door. Intent on surprising her aunt, she tried to open it quietly, but a creaky hinge gave her away. The conversation in the kitchen ceased.

"Hello?" A strong, vibrant voice called out. Sandy couldn't wait any longer. She pushed open the door and stepped into the kitchen.

"Hi," she said.

"Oh my word! Sandy!" Aunty Anne cried, fumbling with her ankle-length dress as she tried to stand. Sandy rushed over and embraced her, revelling for just a moment in the strong embrace she hadn't felt for so long.

"What are you doing here? Why didn't you call?" Aunty Anne asked, near tears.

"I have to let you know I'm coming home now?" Sandy joked. "I thought it would be a nice surprise."

"Well, it definitely is," Aunty Anne said, releasing her.

Sandy turned to the man seated at the small kitchen table, recognizing the square jaw and frazzled white hair instantly. The black and white collar would have given it away to anyone else.

"Hello, Father Savard," Sandy said, reaching in for a hug. Father Savard was a priest from the Manning Catholic Parish, who also held some services out on the reserve.

"So formal, child?" Father Savard replied, in his slight

Québécois accent. "You can call me René."

"That wouldn't feel right," she said, smiling. She turned back to Aunty Anne, who was still struggling to stand up. "What are you doing, Aunty?"

"Getting you some tea. You must be exhausted."

"I can get it," Sandy protested, grabbing a mug from the cupboard and pouring tea from an oversized teapot.

"So," she said, settling into a chair, "why the late-night conference?"

Aunty Anne sighed and took Sandy's hand. "Oh, sweetie. Did you know Lawrence Arcand?"

Sandy thought hard but came up blank. She shook her head.

"Lawrence died last week."

"Oh, no," Sandy said. "How old was he?"

"Fourteen," Father Savard replied, frowning into his teacup.

"Fourteen! That's terrible," Sandy said. "How did it happen?" She had a feeling she already knew the answer.

"The tracks," Father Savard said. "The community is devastated."

"I can't believe this keeps happening." Sandy shook her head. She knew of three schoolmates who had chosen a similar way out when she was growing up. "I saw some kids playing street hockey on the way in," she said. "They didn't look too happy."

"Lawrence is the second young one this year," Aunty Anne said. "It never stops. They're our children. We're supposed to pass on our traditions and beliefs to them, so that they can survive. Instead they choose death."

"Or the Posse," Father Savard said, with a scowl.

"They are one and the same," Aunty Anne said sharply. "Those who join the Posse share nothing with us but blood. Their souls are removed from the Earth that bore us. Their way leads only to a prison cell or death."

Sandy knew all about the Posse. Once just a small gang of

hoodlums, it was now a powerful criminal force. She felt sorry for the many kids who'd been sucked in by the Posse's promises of money, drugs and alcohol. More than one of her friends had fallen in with the gang, only to find out they couldn't get out again.

Sandy had been one of the lucky ones. The Posse had never appealed to her. Nor had the tracks. Instead, inspired by Aunty Anne's use of herbs and plants in traditional healing, Sandy had applied for and gotten a scholarship to the University of Alberta, graduating with a master's degree in botany. She'd always been fascinated with nature's grand design. Each plant, she felt, served a purpose not completely understood. She was trying to find that purpose.

"The reserve has nothing to offer our young people," Father Savard said, finishing his tea. "They ignore the Church. There is nowhere for them to gather, no youth centre. They have no hope, nothing to look forward to."

Aunty Anne nodded. "They need something to do," she said, casting a glance at Sandy. "Some sort of activity, perhaps, to keep them out of trouble."

"Yes." Father Savard nodded. "Perhaps Sandy has some ideas." He got up from the table. "I'd better take my leave," he said. "Let you two lovely ladies catch up." He winked at Sandy. "I'll let myself out."

Sandy collected the mugs from the table. "Why don't you go into the living room," she said to her aunt, "where it's more comfortable. I'll wash up."

It didn't take her long to clear up, and Sandy took a moment to reacquaint herself with the familiar kitchen, the heart of Aunty Anne's home. Nothing much had changed here, either, since she was a kid. The stove and fridge were the same avocado green, the walls the same pale yellow. It even had the same pungent smell from the herbs Aunty Anne used for healing.

It was the smell of Sandy's childhood, of weekend afternoons spent sorting through the morning's haul of leaves and roots, of sick days from school, when Aunty Anne had nursed her back to health. It was the smell of home, where she felt safe, no matter what went on outside the door.

She glanced over to the kitchen wall, which was adorned with charcoal sketches of Native art, one a photo of former Métis senator Thelma Chalifoux, whom Aunty Anne admired. Interspersed were snapshots of family, including childhood photos of Sandy. Her long, straight dark hair. Her slightly crooked nose. Her unsmiling eyes.

God, I was miserable, she thought. She was so lucky to have gotten away. She thought briefly of poor Lawrence Arcand, who had never had the chance to try. Something really did have to be done about it.

Sandy placed the last mug in the cupboard, draped the damp dishtowel over the towel rack and went into the living room. Aunty Anne was sitting in her favourite rocking chair, her head bowed. Sandy smiled. Had she fallen asleep? But no, she could hear her aunt muttering. Sandy hesitated, puzzled then was hit by a sudden realization. This was what Sherry had meant. This was why she had been worried.

Sandy listened for a moment but couldn't make out the words. From what she could hear, they sounded Cree, but she couldn't be sure. She was reaching out to tap Aunty Anne's shoulder when her aunt spoke up.

"It's rude to eavesdrop, dear," she said, with a smile.

"I just wanted to make sure you were okay," Sandy said, trying to keep the worry out of her voice.

"I'm just fine," Aunty Anne said, rubbing her wrists. "Perhaps a bit sore. My joints have been bad the last while."

"I'll get the ointment," Sandy said, retreating to the kitchen and opening the fridge.

"So, what do you think?" Aunty Anne asked from the living room.

About going senile? Sandy wanted to ask. "About what?"

"About the kids. What do you think?"

Sandy pulled an unlabelled jar from the back of the fridge and walked into the living room. "I agree with you—they need something to do."

"Really?" Aunty Anne asked, nodding thankfully as Sandy unscrewed the lid, dipped her fingers in and began gently rubbing the salve into her aunt's wrists and knuckles. "Bless you, my dear."

"It's no different than when I was a kid," Sandy said. "Kids either don't care or aren't interested in learning about their heritage. They need more activities, more...stuff."

Sandy continued working the salve into Aunty Anne's wrinkled skin.

"Like what?" Aunty Anne asked.

Sandy shrugged. "Anything, really. Remember that hockey team we had, when I was a teenager? They played in Manning?"

The hockey team had only lasted a couple of years, disbanding when the Manning Hockey Association raised registration fees. But there was still an interest in hockey in Watishka Lake. Kids had been playing street hockey on the reserve for as long as she could remember. Sandy remembered the kids playing street hockey as she drove in.

"You could start that up again," Sandy said.

"Yes." Aunty Anne nodded. "Or you could."

"Me?" Sandy laughed dismissively. "Yeah, right."

And then a basic principle of botany sprang to mind: *All plants exist within their own ecosystem. Every ecosystem provides plants with what they need to grow.*

"Well, I think I'll be going to bed," Aunty Anne said, capping the jar of salve and pushing herself out of her chair. "Are you coming?"

"I'll call Doug first," Sandy said. "I promised I would."

"Ah yes. That one."

Sandy frowned. "I don't understand why you don't like him, Aunty. He's even Métis."

"I've never met the man who took my daughter thousands of miles away from me," Aunty Anne said, heading for the stairs.

"It was my choice to move with him," Sandy replied sharply.

"Was it?" Aunty Anne turned and smiled, placing a hand on the wooden banister. "Goodnight, *nicânis*. I'm glad you're home."

Sandy watched Aunty Anne mount the stairs, with surprising strength for someone whose joints bothered her so much. She checked her watch and did some math. *Doug will still be awake*, she thought. Aunty Anne's comments had annoyed her a little, but she was used to it. Few on the reserve understood her relationship with Doug.

In her old bedroom, Sandy pulled on one of Doug's old T-shirts and a pair of shorts and tied her hair back in a ponytail, then fell onto the familiar double bed and pulled out her cell phone. She lay for a moment in the darkness and watched the ceiling come alive. Glow-in-the-dark stars ringed the exterior. In the centre was a painting of an eagle feather that Aunty Anne had done for her.

With the threads of an idea forming in her mind, Sandy started to dial.

Chapter Three

Sheldon waited until his parents left for work before rolling out of bed. He was supposed to be at school, but his mom had taken pity on him and let him skip out. He splashed his face with lukewarm water—it never really got hot—pulled on jeans and a hoodie then made his way across the reserve to the trailer park.

The park was a dump. The trailers were 20 to 30 years old, their paint jobs faded, the doors coming unhinged. Dogs ran wild throughout, chasing each other or the rabbits and squirrels that ventured in from the bush. Cars encrusted in snow and rust sat on flat tires in several front yards. Passing one trailer, Sheldon heard a man and a woman yelling obscenities at each other. He imagined it had something to do with the broken liquor bottles on the front steps.

Knowing it was best never to pay too much attention to what happened in this area of the reserve, Sheldon hurried past then ran up the steps of a brown and white corrugated metal trailer and knocked on the door.

He blew on his hands and held them up to his ears, trying to keep them warm, as he waited for someone to come to the door. He regretted now never letting his hair grow, always buzzing it right down to the skin to keep him cool when he was playing.

C'mon, hurry up, he thought. *I'm freezing my butt off out here.*

Finally, Sheldon heard a rustling from the other side of the door and the sound of half a dozen deadbolts being released. The door opened a crack.

"What?" A woman squinted at him through the gap. She was thin, her hair matted, her face and lips covered with sores. Her eyes were ringed with dark circles, and she looked like she hadn't slept in a week. She wore nothing but an oversized T-shirt.

"I'm Lou's brother," Sheldon said. "Is he here?"

"He's sleeping," the woman said. "Do you want to wait?"

Sheldon nodded. The door opened all the way, and Sheldon stepped inside, grateful to be out of the cold.

"I'm Angie," the woman said. The name meant nothing to Sheldon. There was a new woman in Lou's trailer every time he came by.

"Hi," Sheldon said, kicking off his runners.

"I'll try to get him up." Angie yawned and disappeared down the hall.

Sheldon moved farther into the trailer. The place was a pit. He was no neat freak, but every time he came to see his brother, he found it hard to believe that anyone could live not just in this trailer park, but in this filth. The tables and floors were littered with empty beer cans, overflowing ashtrays and leftover scraps of pizza and chips. Dishes were piled on the kitchen counters, and hanging from the back of a chair was a pair of women's panties. Sheldon picked up a small plastic baggie from the floor and sniffed it. Pot.

Lou had offered it to him more than once, but he'd always turned it down, not quite ready to take that step. Sure, he drank and smoked, but drugs were different. It seemed to be what the Posse enjoyed most, though, and Sheldon knew that, when the time came, it was a leap he'd have to make. He'd never admit it, but the idea scared him.

He tossed the baggie onto the coffee table then cleared a spot on the couch and sat down.

Muffled sounds came from the bedroom, and, a moment later, Lou emerged, closing the door behind him. He squinted down the hallway at the front door then at Sheldon. He was clad only in a pair of boxer shorts.

"What's up, bro?" he asked, half sleepily, half...*hung over, most likely,* Sheldon thought.

"Just dropping by," Sheldon said. "Mom and Dad are gone so...I just thought it'd be cool to hang for a bit."

Sheldon only saw his brother when their parents weren't around. Lou had been a problem since he was 11, fighting, smoking and drinking. At 16, he joined the Posse. When their parents found out, they didn't give Lou a choice. Their dad threw Lou out the front door and told him never to come back.

"Yeah." Lou stretched, causing the dark prison tattoos to ripple across his biceps. Like Sheldon, Lou was skinny, thanks, probably, to his seedy lifestyle. But that's where the resemblance ended. Though his brother was five years older than Sheldon, Lou was the shorter of the two. Unlike Sheldon, Lou kept his hair long, and his face was pocked with acne scars and sores. And, although Sheldon had broken his nose playing hockey, it was Lou who'd seen tougher days—there were scars and burns on his chest, stomach and arms, some fresher than others.

"How was jail?" Sheldon asked.

Lou shrugged, reaching for a nearby pack of cigarettes. "The usual. Got into some stuff, but nothing I couldn't handle.

Cellmate was quiet, so that was good."

Lou lit a cigarette, offering the pack to Sheldon, who took one. He lit Sheldon's cigarette, then reached into a pile of silver rings on the table and started placing them on his fingers. The rings, sporting skulls and studs, didn't quite cover the letters tattooed on his fingers: P-O-S-S-E.

"How was GP?" Lou asked, taking a deep drag on his cigarette. "You make it?"

Sheldon shrugged, trying to deflect the anger that surged through him whenever he thought about it.

"That's crap." Lou picked up a pair of jeans off the floor and examined them before pulling them on. Then he found a wrinkled white undershirt and put that on, too.

"Their loss," he said, holding the cigarette between his teeth as he tucked the shirt into his jeans. He grinned. "But our gain."

"Yeah," Sheldon said. "They want some softy team, they can have it."

"So, what are you gonna do?" Lou asked, through a haze of smoke.

Sheldon shrugged. "Just get back on with the team in Manning, I guess."

"You're spinning your wheels there, man."

"No choice now," Sheldon said, poking idly at an empty beer can with his toe. "Gotta play."

Lou went into the kitchen and opened the fridge. "You want a brew?"

Sheldon nodded. A can of beer shot through the air and landed in his lap. Sheldon tapped the top of the can three times then cracked it open. No spray. It was early, but he took a deep swig. It tasted good.

Lou put his beer down on the table, pulled a red bandana off the back of a chair, and tied it around his forehead.

"You don't have to play," Lou said.

Sheldon nodded, swallowing a mouthful of beer.

"I got you covered. You're 16 in a month. You're in like flint, bro."

"I know," Sheldon said.

"You follow me, you could rule this place."

Sheldon thought about it. It was tempting. No worries, no cares, no responsibilities. It meant staying in Watishka Lake, but, really, what other choice did he have? Getting cut in GP had shattered his lifelong dream, and now...now, he had no dreams. He sniffed absently, blinking back sudden tears. Sheldon quickly looked away, so his brother didn't see. He had to show Lou he was tough.

"What do I have to do?" he asked, after a pause.

Lou laughed, butting out his cigarette. "That's a part of it, bro. You find out then. It's a secret, part of the initiation."

"I'm your brother."

"And I still can't tell you." As Lou reached for his beer, a cell phone resting on the table started vibrating. He grabbed it, checked the text message then rubbed his face tiredly. "Gotta go."

"Where?" Sheldon downed the last of his beer. The buzz had helped take the edge off his anger.

"Can't tell you that, either." Lou pulled on a black leather jacket and pocketed his wallet and keys then reached under the kitchen sink and grabbed a black backpack. "You can hang out here if you want, party a bit. Angie's cool."

"I'll just go home." Sheldon stood.

"All right," Lou said, sliding shiny aviator sunglasses onto his pockmarked face. Sheldon could see himself in them—angry, resentful, his face drawn and sad. He followed Lou out the door and watched as his brother used a ring of keys to lock the deadbolts.

Lou threw an arm around Sheldon's shoulder and pulled him close.

"Don't forget," he whispered.

"I won't," Sheldon said. He watched as Lou walked to his car, an old rust-boat, one long trip away from breaking down. Sheldon turned in the opposite direction, striking off for home in the dim, grey cold.

Cody inhaled the cold night air, skating as best he could by the light of the three-quarter moon. He'd cleared the small patch on the creek soon after winter set in and had diligently shovelled it after each snowfall. On bright nights, like this one, when the sky was clear and the stars shone with a hard brilliance, he was out here, skating. Sometimes, he even skated by the shifting, shimmering light of the aurora.

The aurora was streaking the sky green tonight. As Cody looked up at the dancing light, his skate caught in a rut and he fell, pain exploding across his stomach on impact. Immediately, he picked himself up and dug his skates back into the ice.

Cody had been on his way home from school when the Posse car lurched to a halt in front of him. The passenger's side door had opened, and the one person Cody had been trying to avoid all week emerged—Alicia.

"Cody!" She got right in his face, so he had no choice but to talk to her. Her eyes were dark, empty holes, her skin sickly pale. She looked like she hadn't bathed in a week.

"It wasn't my fault," she said.

Cody had been wondering what he'd say if this moment ever came. He'd never settled on an answer. What came out was simple and biting.

"Yeah, it was, Alicia," he said. It felt good.

Alicia had looked at him like he'd shot her, then her expression quickly twisted into one of anger.

"You're such a loser," she said, as if that were all the intellectual strength she could muster. "You're just like him."

Cody had smiled, oddly enough. "Better him than you," he said.

Alicia spun on her heel and climbed back into the car. He watched it, with a thrill of satisfaction, as it roared off down the road.

But, as he'd trudged home, that satisfaction had faded. He could make Alicia cry a million times over, but it wouldn't change anything. Lawrence was still gone, and picking on someone like her didn't change that, even if it felt good.

With the memory of his friend foremost in his mind, Cody continued to skate.

"I like your idea," Aunty Anne said. She and Sandy were sitting in the kitchen, breakfasting on toast and homemade Saskatoon-berry jam.

"Really?" Sandy asked. "Something as simple as a hockey team?"

"Sometimes the simple ideas are the best ones," Aunty Anne said, absent-mindedly rubbing her wrists. "And everyone we've talked to seems to like it."

Sandy poured hot water into the teapot and brought it and two mugs over to the table. The idea had coalesced in her head over the last few days, and before she knew it, she was scribbling out her plan on a notepad.

"And the band council meets tomorrow night?" Sandy asked.

Aunty Anne nodded. "Should be interesting. The chief hasn't seen you in years."

"And the families and kids will come?"

"I guarantee it."

Sandy took a bite of toast and mulled over her plan. Had she covered everything? What was missing? Her mind came up blank.

"What does Doug think?" Aunty Anne asked.

"Doug? He's a hockey player. He thinks it's the greatest idea ever."

Chapter Four

Chief Alexander Bullchild had never seen so many people at a council meeting before. Nor so many kids. What was going on?

He and his four councillors had just taken their seats at the front. The normally empty chairs were filled with parents and children, and some were even standing along the walls. There were more than a hundred people in attendance, far more than usual.

Chief Bullchild banged his gavel on the mantel, to signal the beginning of the meeting. He was about to speak, when he spotted a face in the crowd.

Sandy Lafonde. How long had it been?

Sandy was sitting near the front of the crowd, nervously bending back the corners of a notebook on her lap.

"Is there anyone in the gallery who wishes to address council?" Chief Bullchild asked, surveying the crowd.

"Yes."

The Chief watched in surprise as Sandy stood and walked

to the lectern. "Ms. Lafonde." He nodded at her. "Welcome home."

Sandy cleared her throat then leaned into the microphone. She'd spent all day writing down exactly what she wanted to say. Still, her hands shook as she flipped the pages of her notebook. "We have a problem on the reserve," she said. "And I think there's a way we can do something about it." There was some muttering from the councillors, but Sandy ignored it and kept talking. Her eyes never leaving her notebook, she recited every word she had written down. Her speech took a little less than four minutes.

"So let me get this straight," Chief Bullchild said, when she was done. "You think starting up a local hockey team will solve the problems we're having with our young people? That seems a little…simplistic."

"It would be a start. It would give teenagers something to identify with," Sandy replied.

There were some murmurs of agreement from the crowd, and Sandy could see heads nodding. Encouraged, she went on. "We're not asking for much. We need ice to skate on, obviously. And we need some equipment."

There was silence from the council table. Then a young councillor—Raymond Ouellette—spoke up. Aunty Anne had warned Sandy about him—he was cocky, educated and out of touch with his people, she'd said. Rumour was that Ouellette was concerned with serving a higher office—as an MP—and that a council seat was just a step in that direction.

"Ms. Lafonde," he said pompously, "while your intentions are certainly admirable, the budget for the coming year has already been set."

Sandy had been ready for this. She'd heard from many residents that this was a boys' club, whose members did what they pleased. New ideas were frowned upon. She forged ahead.

"I understand that," Sandy replied, her voice calm but determined. "But surely there is something you can do to help. This is our children's future we're talking about. One of them laid down on the railroad tracks not long ago and let a train end his life because he didn't feel he had a future here." The thought suddenly angered her, and her voice began to rise.

"He's not the first," she continued, "and he won't be the last. If it's not suicide, it's the Posse. If it's not the Posse, then they just run away. Yes, some go to school, but how many come back? Most have nothing to keep them here! Nothing!"

"I'd like to speak," a voice broke in. Everett Strawberry, the oldest member of council, raised his hand. He turned his attention to Sandy, who was struggling to regain her composure.

"Ms. Lafonde, let's say, hypothetically speaking, that we could provide some ice for your team. What else would you need?"

"We'd need nets," Sandy said. Something like hope rose in her chest.

"I got some old lumber and chicken wire I'm not using," a man near the back volunteered.

"What about skates? Sticks? Pucks?" Strawberry pressed.

"We can probably buy pucks...." Sandy frowned. "But you're right. When it comes to sticks and skates, that's where we need help."

There was a pause, as Strawberry scribbled some notes on a pad of paper. "Chief Bullchild, we have a water-pumper truck sitting idle at the moment, don't we?"

"We do," the Chief conceded.

"Then, why don't we help the community with this hockey team?" Strawberry asked. "This is one of the best ideas I've heard in this chamber. I think we can come up with a few hundred dollars to buy some sticks. And as for skates, we can provide those, too. If you look in a certain storage locker in the public works building, Ms. Lafonde, you'll find four or five boxes of skates, left over from a team we organized for the boys some time ago."

The councillor looked up at Sandy. "What about a coach?" he asked.

Sandy blanked. That was the one thing she hadn't thought of. "We don't have one," she said, her spirits sinking.

"Actually, I think I know someone who could do it, someone the kids can relate to." This time, it was Chief Bullchild who spoke up. "I'll give him a call right after we're done."

"Shall we put it to a vote, then?" Strawberry asked. Four hands went up in favour.

"Ms. Lafonde, you have your hockey team," the Chief said.

Sheldon was lying on his bed, staring at the cracks in the ceiling. He was thinking about his future. For the first time in his life, it was obscured, hazy, like smoke. His hockey skills were supposed to take him all the way to the NHL. Now he was going nowhere. What was he going to do?

His next best bet was joining his brother's gang. He didn't know or understand half of what Lou and the rest of the Posse did, but how bad could it be? *Gotta be better than wasting my time here*, he thought.

There was a knock at the door.

"What?"

Sheldon's father poked his head into the room. "You've got a phone call," he said, tossing Sheldon the cordless phone. "It's your uncle."

"What does he want?" Sheldon hoped the Chief didn't want to talk about his getting cut from the team. It seemed like everyone in his family had been riding on Sheldon's chance in Grande Prairie.

"Ask him yourself," his dad said, as he left the room.

Sheldon picked up the phone. "Hey, Chief."

"Hey, buddy! Sorry to hear about the team."

"I don't wanna talk about it."

"I didn't think so," the Chief replied. "I was calling to offer you a chance to do something special for Watishka Lake. You're the only person who can do it."

Sheldon rolled his eyes. He didn't want to help the reserve. He wanted to leave. "What have you got in mind?" he asked cautiously.

"How do you feel about coaching a hockey team?"

Sheldon sat up. "What are you talking about?"

Forty minutes later, Sheldon hung up the phone, thinking over what he'd just agreed to. He was going to coach the Watishka Lake hockey team. Better still, he was also going to play.

He knew he would be the best player on the team. But the coaching part, that was the kicker. It was his chance to show everyone that he could be part of a team. Maybe they'd get a game somewhere, and maybe, just maybe, someone would notice him. He'd get a second chance.

Sandy couldn't stop sneezing. The dust was everywhere.

She'd shown up at the public works building, where an employee in blue coveralls was waiting for her.

"Boxes should be in the crawl space under the stairs," the man said, handing her a flashlight. "No power in there."

After unlocking the door and giving her curt instructions for locking up again, the man climbed into a banged-up truck and drove away.

The crawl space was packed with boxes and crates, most of them containing old tools, greasy rags and boxes of papers and photos. She peered into the darkness, the contents of the room illuminated only by her flashlight. She pulled down boxes, rummaged through them then pushed them out into the hallway. Despite the cold, she was sweating.

After half an hour, Sandy reached into a box and felt her fingers graze leather. She kept probing and touched laces then the cold steel of skate blades. Encouraged, she pulled the box out into the open and looked inside. *Bingo!*

The skates were old, there was no doubt about that, and some of them were singles, but Sandy didn't care. She grabbed another nearby box, opened it and found exactly the same contents. When she was finished sorting them out, Sandy had four boxes of hockey skates.

She reached farther back, looking for anything else that might be there, and felt canvas. She recognized the feeling—and the smell—almost immediately. She grabbed and pulled, freeing the hockey bag from its enclosure. Hauling it out into the hallway, Sandy put the flashlight between her teeth and pulled on the rusted zipper. Slowly, the contents revealed themselves.

It's all here, she thought gleefully. The bag contained one full set of goalie equipment, complete with mask, pads, chest protector, catcher, blocker and even an enormous jock strap.

Well, a goalie would need one, she giggled to herself then started hauling the bag and boxes out to her SUV. She had a lot to do. She wanted to drop the skates off at the Auger house, where Robert, a jack-of-all-trades, would use his grinder to remove the rust and sharpen the skates as best he could. Then she needed to dash to Manning to pick up laces, tape, hockey sticks and, if there was enough money left over, as many pucks as she could find.

She was just pulling away from the public works yard, when a bright light caught her eye. She followed the road to its source and saw another public works employee dwarfed by an enormous water-pumper truck. A portable light connected to a generator illuminated the tiny droplets of water as they gushed from the pumper's hose and cascaded over a large, flat patch of ground that had been scraped free of snow.

It's really happening, Sandy thought, as she watched the water freeze almost on contact with the thin layer of ice already forming on the ground. She looked around and was thrilled to see a pair of wooden benches placed at one side of the rink. At each end, resting on top of the snow, was a net, made from scrap lumber and chicken wire.

For a moment, Sandy thought she saw someone in the brush at the far end of the rink. She blinked, but the figure was gone.

It's all coming together, she thought.

In the bushes, the old man clutched his walking stick and peered out to see what was going on.

It was about time.

He felt eyes in his direction and drew back into the bush then vanished into the trees.

"Everything went perfectly!" Sandy announced, as she burst in the door.

The house was quiet.

"Aunty Anne?" Sandy removed her coat and boots and crossed into the dimly lit living room.

Her aunt, dressed in a flannel nightgown, was sitting in her favourite chair. Her head was bowed, her eyes closed, her lips moved quickly and quietly.

Sandy's heart sank. It was happening again.

Minding Aunty Anne's warning about "eavesdropping," Sandy stepped back out of the living room and made her way to her bedroom. Tomorrow was going to be a big day.

Anne heard the creak of footsteps then gingerly opened her right eye to watch Sandy disappear up the stairs. She smiled.

It's working, she said silently in Cree.

The response came quickly and quietly.

She'll understand her purpose in time.

Chapter Five

Cody was up before the sun. He'd dressed in the dark, throwing on a warm sweater and long johns under a pair of sweatpants.

Now he was eating breakfast, scooping Cheerios into his mouth between glances at the clock hanging on the kitchen wall. Underneath his chair, his feet were gyrating excitedly.

"Someone's up early," his mother said softly, passing into the tiny but tidy kitchen and stooping to kiss Cody's unkempt hair.

"I can't wait!" Cody said, gulping cereal. "I want to get out there."

Eileen spied the small gym bag by the door.

"You have your skates?"

"Yup. I hope they have some sticks, though. Mine's not good enough."

Cody could skate a bit, and he could shoot a little, too, but his stick was only good for road hockey. It was a broken shaft he'd found in a dumpster. Screwed onto it was a plastic blade he'd bought with his allowance money. It wasn't much of a stick, but until now, it had been enough.

"What if I'm not good enough?" he asked.

"You're going to do just fine," his mother said. "You can already skate. You're miles ahead of everyone else."

"I could be better."

"And you'll get better," his mother replied.

"Can I go?" Cody asked, pushing his chair away from the table.

"You don't want a ride?"

"Naw. It's not that far. Plus, I told Nicky and Stan I'd walk over with them."

"All right." His mom smiled at him. "Just come right home afterwards. I want to hear all about it."

Cody pushed open the back door. Nicky and Stan were waiting for him outside. "You guys ready?"

"Hell, yeah!" Nicky replied, greeting Cody with a high five. Stan held up his meaty hand, and they traded a few smacks. Cody was the only one holding a bag.

"No skates?" he asked.

"They got skates for us there," Stan huffed, his heavy parka making him look even bigger than he was. Cody couldn't get used to how big Stan was now. He hadn't just gotten taller, like most of the kids at school; he'd also bulked up.

"I hear they even got some goalie stuff, too," Stan said.

"I ain't playing goalie," Nicky said.

"Me neither," Cody added. "I'm playing forward, just like Sidney Crosby. I'm going straight for the net." He took a few skating strides then swung an imaginary stick. "In on goal... Gladue scores!"

"You can't skate like Crosby," Nicky said, giving Cody a shove. Nicky was shorter than Cody, but he was scrappy. He was always poking or shoving people, even Stan—and most guys knew better than to mess with Stan, not because he was mean, but because one swing of his beefy arm could send you to the hospital. Nicky never meant any harm by it, though—at least, most of the time he didn't.

"You can barely skate," Nicky said. "None of us can really skate."

"I can skate," Cody replied. "I can skate better than you two slugs. And, besides, do you know who our coach is gonna be?" Nicky and Stan shook their heads.

"Sheldon! Sheldon's gonna be our coach! He's gonna teach us how to be just as good as he is!" Cody could barely contain his excitement. On the reserve, Sheldon was as close to a star as you could get, at least to Cody.

Cody had watched Sheldon play in Manning. On days when his mom went into town, Cody hung out at the rink to catch whatever teams were playing. He'd seen Sheldon play dozens of times, and he always managed to do something new and exciting. He seemed to dangle on the very edge of his skate blades, knowing exactly which way to go to evade a defenseman and which shot to take to score another one of his hundreds of goals. Though Cody cheered for Sidney Crosby and the Pittsburgh Penguins whenever they were on *Hockey Night in Canada*, Sheldon Lambert was his real hero.

And now he was going to be coaching them.

They stopped at the main road that bisected the reserve, watching for traffic, then ran across.

"I don't know," Stan said, frowning. "I heard Sheldon just got cut from some team in GP. Why's he gonna coach us?"

"Because he needs something to do, stupid," Nicky retorted. "He may as well teach the rest of us, so maybe we have a chance."

"Yeah," Stan said, scratching at the short, dark hair under his toque. "But Sheldon's gonna be 16 pretty soon, I heard. And his brother..." Stan's voice trailed off.

Cody knew what he meant. Lou was what Cody's mom called a "nasty piece of work."

"I'd never join the Posse," Cody said.

"You wanna stay here?" Nicky asked incredulously.

"I don't know," Cody said, tromping through the snow. "If I was going to leave Watishka Lake, I'd rather be something...you know?"

"Guys." Stan touched their shoulders and pointed. "Look."

Just across the field, surrounded by a ridge of snow, an enormous expanse of ice glistened in the sunlight. At each end was a net, and cutting across the middle of the ice were two bluelines and one redline, painted in bright colours.

"Wow," Cody said, awed by the size of the rink. "Look at that!"

"It's like in Manning," Stan said. "But outside."

"There's no boards," Nicky said, frowning.

"Maybe we'll get those later," Stan said.

"C'mon guys." Cody took off, running. "Last one there plays goalie!"

Although they covered the intervening distance in a matter of seconds, they weren't the first ones to the rink. A small group of kids was already milling around, some stepping onto the ice in their shoes to slide around. A few vehicles idled off to the side, as parents, unwilling to venture out into the cold, watched their children from a distance.

"Hey, Cody!" a boy sliding on the ice called out. It was Billy "Little Buffalo" Chalifoux, one of Cody's friends from school. Billy came by his traditional name honestly—he was huge, thanks to his fondness for tortilla chips and video games. In truth, Cody was surprised to see him out on the ice at all.

"You gonna play, Billy?" Cody asked, as he approached the ice.

"I don't know," Billy said, lining up his next slide. "My dad made me come. Said it would be good for me. And hockey's okay."

Billy took a few preparatory steps then exploded forward, running quickly before stopping and letting his momentum carry him across the ice. Suddenly, he lost his balance and started flailing his arms in the air to get it back. It didn't work, and, before anyone could help, Billy fell, butt first, onto the ice.

"Wow! The ice didn't break!" a voice jeered. Cody turned and came face to face with Garry Saddleback, a kid from school he usually tried to avoid. Garry was 15, a year older than Cody, but in the same grade. He was tall and lanky, and he spent most of his time in the school bathroom, admiring his hair. He was also mean to pretty much everyone around him.

"Up yours, Garry," Nicky retorted. "Why don't you go to the hairdresser with your Mom and get your hair curled?"

There was a sudden silence, as everyone turned to look at Garry, whose face had turned purple.

"Oh, that's right. You can't. Your Mom's in JAIL!" Nicky shouted.

"Shut up, toothpick!" Garry hurled himself at Nicky, tackling him to the ground and throwing punches with his fists. It didn't last long. Stan reached out and grabbed Garry by the hair, pulling forcefully.

"Get off him, Garry," Stan said quietly.

Garry obliged, gritting his teeth as Stan pulled him to his feet by the hair then shoved him away.

"You fight like a girl," Garry said to Nicky.

"You dress like one," Nicky said, standing up.

"That's enough, boys!" a woman's voice called out. Cody looked up and saw a short, pretty woman approaching the rink. It was Sandy Lafonde, Aunty Anne's daughter. She'd appeared out of the blue a few days ago. Now she was organizing the team. Father Savard was with her.

"Let's get you guys set up," she said, smiling. "Come on."

Cody and the others fell quickly into line, as Sandy led the way toward the wooden benches and instructed them to take a seat. Cody found a spot and began to scan the benches, checking out his new teammates while he waited for his turn. At one end of the bench, sitting next to Nicky and Stan, was scrawny Paul Lacroix, who was only 12 and looked like he could tread water in a garden hose. Next to him was Matthew Loonskin, whose nickname was Pizza Face because of his acne. Sitting next to Matt was Andy Saddleback, Garry's cousin, shivering in a sweater and windbreaker. Cody felt sorry for him. No one on the reserve had a lot of money, but Andy's parents were in a pretty bad way. Andy once admitted that they sometimes had to choose between food and clothes, though they could somehow always afford liquor. Last but not least, hunkered down at the end, was Billy. Crowded onto the other bench were the Cardinal twins, Teddy and Tyler and some kids Cody didn't know very well.

Cody looked around for Sheldon but saw no sign of the coach. He was nervous about meeting his idol.

"Let's do skates first," Sandy said, pulling a box out of the back of her SUV and handing it off to Father Savard, who had ditched his priest's collar in favour of a blue and gold hockey jersey that read "Holy Rollers."

"These skates are old, but they're still good," Sandy said, handing another box to Father Savard. "We might not have them in your exact size, but we'll do the best we can."

Sandy and Father Savard worked their way along the benches, asking each boy for his shoe size then digging into the box to find what they could. In some cases, the skates were a size too big, in others, a half size too small. Few fit perfectly.

Sandy and Father Savard were halfway down the line of players when a sudden commotion from across the field caused everyone to look up. A Chrysler Daytona, spewing black smoke, was coming up the road, travelling in reverse. Music boomed from the car.

"Oh great," Nicky groaned, trying to worm his size-9 foot into a size-8 skate.

Cody looked up eagerly. Their coach had finally arrived.

"You don't have to do this, bro." Lou looked over his shoulder from the front seat. He had a cigarette tucked behind one ear.

Sheldon shrugged, checking out the line of kids who were struggling with their second-hand skates. None of the kids seemed to know what they were doing. He was already wondering if this was a good idea.

"At least I can play," he said. "And coach."

"And these little punks will be a challenge?"

Sheldon smirked. "They'll make *me* look good."

Lou pulled his sunglasses down and stared at Sheldon over the rims.

"You don't have long to wait," he said. "Just stick with me and everything'll be cool before you know it. We're brothers. We'll be even more later."

"I know, Lou," Sheldon said. "And I'm stoked. But I got to do something until then."

He glanced up at their driver, an overweight Cree from a reserve to the south. A skull earring hung from his left earlobe. He stared out the front window of the vehicle through wrap-around sunglasses and stroked a sparse goatee. There was an unmistakable bulge in his leather jacket. He made Sheldon nervous.

"All right, bro," Lou said, reaching back with his hand. "Stay cool."

Sheldon reached forward and wrapped his fingers around his brother's. Their eyes met for just a second, then Sheldon threw open the door, pulling his skates and stick behind him. He had just reached the benches when he heard his brother's voice call out.

"Hey, ladies!" Lou yelled. "Bet you can't hit this!"

Sheldon smirked as everyone stared at the car roaring backwards down the road, a pair of bum cheeks pressed against the windshield.

Chapter Six

"Lame," Nicky said, rolling his eyes as the car sped away.

"Whatever," Billy said, still waiting for skates. "Just a bunch of no-good punks."

Cody didn't reply. He was trying not to stare at Sheldon, resisting the urge to run up and introduce himself.

"Hey, guys." Sheldon offered up a half-smile and a wave. "I'm Sheldon. I'll be playing on your team and coaching."

No one said anything.

"We're just getting everyone ready," Sandy said. "We only have one pair of skates left. And they're these."

She held up a pair of skates, laces intertwined, with one finger, but these were different from the rest. Though every other pair of skates looked old and beaten, the pair she held looked like skates set inside plastic boots. She held them out to Billy.

"What are those?" he asked, frowning.

"These, *nitotem*," Sandy replied, "are goalie skates."

"Why would I wear goalie skates?" Billy asked.

"Because…" Sheldon sauntered over and eyed Billy up and down. "You are going to be our goalie."

"What? No way!" Billy protested. "Goalies are crazy. I'll get hurt!"

"You won't get hurt," Sandy said. "We have a full set of pads and gloves and everything for you. You'll be protected."

"But I don't know how to play goalie!"

"Doesn't matter," Sheldon said casually. "You'll take up half the net. All you have to do is stand there."

Billy flinched. Behind Sheldon, a few eyes widened.

"Fine," he said angrily, grabbing the skates.

"Let me know if you can't bend over to tie them up," Sheldon added as he walked away. "We'll get your Mommy out here to do it for you."

"What a jerk," Nicky whispered.

"Maybe he's just trying to motivate us," Cody suggested.

"Sure is a crappy way of doing it."

Sheldon took a seat on a mound of snow and started lacing up his own skates. When he was done, he grabbed his hockey gloves, pulled a whistle on a lanyard over his head and skated onto the ice, stick in hand.

He stopped and turned. The players were still struggling into their skates.

"Are you ladies almost done?" Sheldon bellowed.

"Sheldon, could you wait a moment, please?" Sandy asked. "A lot of these kids have never worn skates before."

"Whatever." Sheldon rolled his eyes. He pulled a puck from his jacket pocket and started stickhandling deftly across the ice.

It took another few minutes for the players to lace up their skates, except for Billy, who was not only putting on skates but also shoulder pads, a chest pad, leg pads and gloves.

One at a time, the players stepped tentatively onto the ice. Garry and Stan got as far as the snow bordering the rink then tripped and fell face first. Nicky and Matt just made it off the bench. Only Cody actually made it onto the ice and stayed upright. He took a few experimental strides on the new ice. Compared to the bumpy, rutted creek, it felt amazing.

"This isn't going to work," Billy moaned. He was lying face-down in the snow while Sandy fastened his leg pads as tightly as they would go.

"You're going to do just fine," Sandy clucked cheerfully.

"That's not what I meant."

She helped Billy to his feet then turned and called to the others. "Okay, come get your sticks!" The rush that ensued almost caused injuries, as the players stumbled toward Sandy in eager anticipation. Nicky, in the middle of the pack, hit a rut in the ice as he tried to slow down and fell on his side. The players behind him, most of whom didn't know how to stop, had nowhere to go. Sandy watched in horror as eight of the team's players fell to the ice like bowling pins. A series of moans and groans erupted from the pile as each skater struggled to his feet.

"You've gotta be freakin' kidding me," Sheldon muttered.

Sandy caught Sheldon's eye and beckoned him over. He shrugged then swooped in, showering Sandy in a flurry of ice shavings as he skidded to a stop.

"Most of these guys haven't played hockey before," she explained.

"No shit," Sheldon said, rolling his eyes.

Sandy frowned. "Listen, you're going to have to be patient with them," she said, trying not to lose her own temper. "They need to learn, and they need to have fun."

"Don't worry. I'll learn 'em," Sheldon said. He skated away, snapped a puck up on his stick and slapped it into the centre of the net.

The players had finally staggered to their feet and were now crowding around the pile of sticks in the snow next to the benches. Sandy asked them to line up, then each player stepped forward to receive his stick.

Cody looked over his in wonder. It was black with white writing, and scrawled on one side was a replica autograph. The name and number were unmistakable.

Sidney Crosby, #87.

"Awesome," Cody whispered. He reached out with the blade and teased a chunk of snow onto the rink. Crouching low, he snapped his wrists forward. The chunk of snow disintegrated as it skittered along the ice, coming to rest just wide of the goal.

With each player properly equipped, Sandy turned to a white bucket that she had kept hidden behind one of the benches. She'd had just enough money left, after buying sticks, new laces and tape, for the bucket and its contents. She ripped the top off the bucket and poured 30 pucks onto the ice.

"Now, everyone keep an eye on these, because they are all we have," she said, as the players headed for the pucks. "If you shoot one off the ice, go find it. At the end of practice, make sure each puck goes back in the bucket."

Cody was reaching for a puck when a shrill whistle pierced the air. He turned. Sheldon was standing at centre ice, whistle in his teeth, arms wrapped casually around his stick.

"No pucks yet," he said. "We have some work to do first. Everyone down to the far side and line up along the goal line." He pointed to the far end of the rink with his stick. One at a time, some stumbling, some tripping, the players slowly made their way down the ice.

"Billy!" Sheldon yelled. "Get over here!"

"Why?" Billy was sitting on the bench. He'd hardly moved, but his face was dripping with sweat. "I'm the goalie. I don't have to skate."

"Yes, you do," Sheldon replied.

"Says who?"

"Says me! Get over here now!"

Billy grumbled but pushed himself to his feet then grabbed the goal stick and stepped gingerly onto the ice. His legs encumbered by the bulky pads, he shuffled gingerly across the ice to the goal line.

"Skate, don't walk," Sheldon yelled.

"I'm trying," Billy whined. The thick skates were awkward, and the blades didn't bite into the ice. Eventually, he reached the goal line, letting his weight bring him to a very slow stop. Using his stick almost as a cane, Billy turned around to face Sheldon.

"Wow." Sheldon was staring at his wrist, even though he wasn't wearing a watch. "New record for slowest time ever. From now on, when I tell you guys to do something, you do it as fast as you can, got it?"

Sheldon turned back to the others. "All right, when I blow my whistle, I want you guys to skate as fast you can to the other end. Okay?"

The players nodded.

"Okay." Sheldon skated backwards to centre ice and came to a stop. He paused briefly then blew one sharp whistle.

His heart sank. He could see only one kid who knew how to skate. The rest were leaning on their sticks for support, slowly making their way across the rink. Some shuffled their feet, their skate blades never leaving the ice. Others were doing little more than running in their skates, arms wind-milling furiously as they tried to stay upright.

Cody reached the end of the rink just as the rest of the pack reached centre ice. He skidded to a stop and turned, his face beaming with pride at being the fastest skater on the team. His smile slowly evaporated as he watched the rest head toward him. They were picking up speed, but none of them knew how to stop. Cody turned and scooted as fast as he could to the side of the ice.

Sheldon watched with a mounting sense of frustration, as all but one of the players reached the far end of the rink. Instead of coming to a stop, however, they careened into the border of snow and fell into a heap. Sheldon groaned. These guys were lame! He was usually the star on any team, but at least the players around him knew how to skate. He wasn't sure what he'd expected, but it wasn't this. He was starting to wonder if he'd gotten a raw deal. He blew the whistle.

"That's the best you can do?" he asked incredulously.

The players were still pushing themselves to their feet. Stan finally spoke up.

"No one ever taught us how to skate."

"Well, that's obvious." Sheldon sighed. "Watch me." He made his way to one side of the rink, parallel to his players. "You go like this." Slowly and deliberately, Sheldon pushed his left skate into the ice then his right then his left. He covered the distance from side to side in six easy strides.

"Got it?"

There were a few nods, including one from the kid who could skate.

"All right. On the whistle, hard as you can to the other side. Go!"

The whistle blew. The result was the same—14 players writhing in the snow bank at the far end.

"Okay, we can work on that later," Sheldon said, gritting his teeth. "Let's try it going backwards."

"Backwards? We can barely skate forwards, and you want us to go backwards?" Nicky squawked.

"Here, watch me." Sheldon skated to the far end of the rink and, swooping his blades in large C's, skated backwards up the ice. "Got it?"

"What did you just do?" Billy asked.

"I just…" Sheldon stalled, fumbling for words. He didn't know how to explain what he had just done. He just knew how to do it. "Here, watch again."

Sheldon skated backwards again to the far end of the rink and back again. He looked at the players. They looked back, confused.

"Do I have to do this?" Billy asked.

"Yes! Goalies have to skate backwards," Sheldon said, struggling to maintain his cool. "On the whistle…Go!"

The whistle screeched. The players turned slowly on the tips of their skate blades and started moving backwards. After one step, four had fallen. The rest were shuffling in reverse, focused more on staying upright than actually skating.

Sheldon was ready to give up, when he noticed that one player hadn't fallen and was actually skating backwards. It was the same kid who had skated so well earlier. Sheldon skated over to him.

"What's your name?" he asked.

The kid seemed nervous. "Cody."

"Cody? You're doing good out there. You're going to be one of my defensemen."

"But I was hoping to play forward!" Cody protested. "Sidney Crosby's my hero. I want to play like him."

"Kid, you're the only one who knows how to skate backwards," Sheldon replied. "You're playing defence." He skated away, leaving Cody feeling crushed.

Sheldon turned back to the others and wished he hadn't. They'd made little progress. The best skaters had made it to the near blueline, but most had just given up and were sprawled on the ice. Sheldon scowled. This was a stupid idea. Why had he let the Chief talk him into it? No one had told him these stupid kids didn't even know how to skate.

"Never mind! We'll work on that later," Sheldon shouted.

"Let's see if you can shoot." He looked around. "Where's the fat kid?"

"It's Billy," Billy said forcefully. He said some other things, too, but not loudly enough for Sheldon to hear.

"Whatever. Get in the net."

"And do what?" Billy asked.

"Stop pucks, smart guy. What do you think?" Sheldon said.

"But I don't know how!"

"Do I have to show you guys EVERYTHING?" Sheldon fumed. "Here. You stand like this." Sheldon put his knees together then crouched over them, his knees bent. He held his stick in one hand between his skates and the other in the air. "Then you move and try to stop the puck."

"How do I stop the puck?" Billy asked.

"However you want! Butterfly! Pad stack! Stick save! Whatever!" Sheldon gestured furiously at the net with his stick. "Get in there!"

Billy shuffled toward the net. "I don't know what any of those things are," he grumbled. He skated into the freshly painted crease, turned around, then reached up and pulled the mask over his face. When he looked up, his blood froze. The players were lined up facing him, and each one had a puck.

"All right. One at a time."

Nicky stepped up first. Though his shot travelled less than half the distance to the goal, Billy had immediately put his blocker and catcher over his face.

"It didn't even hit you, ya big chicken!" Sheldon yelled. "All right. Next."

Andy shot next. He snapped his wrists so hard, he fell onto his stomach, but the puck skittered down the ice all the way to the goal. Billy watched it pass by his right skate and stop with a thunk at the back of the net.

"Right on!" Andy pumped his fist, accepting high-fives from Nicky and a few other players.

"Billy!" Sheldon yelled. "You're supposed to stop the puck!"

"I didn't know how."

Sheldon grumbled. There was only one way he was going to get Billy used to the puck.

"Fine!" he said, grabbing a puck for himself. "Everyone aim and shoot when I blow my whistle."

"Everyone?" Billy asked, but it was too late. The whistle sounded, and a dozen pucks came flying at him. Billy fell to his knees, as three-quarters of the shots actually made their way to the net, some bouncing off his pads.

"Oh, for God's sake," Sheldon fumed. He pushed the puck a few feet ahead of him, took two strides and sent a blistering slapshot screaming toward Billy. It caromed off the side of his facemask and bounced off the ice. Billy promptly collapsed onto the ice.

Chapter Seven

Sheldon skated over to Billy and stood looking down at him. "Did that hurt?" he asked.

"Yes!" Billy said, through clenched teeth. Tears filled his eyes. He'd already discarded his gloves and was prying at his face-mask to get it off. Sandy was making her way across the ice.

"Remember this—that's the worst thing that can happen to you in that equipment," Sheldon said, as Sandy knelt and took Billy's head in her hands.

"Let me know when he's ready," Sheldon growled. "All right, everyone down to the other end and we'll keep practicing. There's no goalie, but that won't make a difference."

The rest of the team skated off, leaving Sandy and Billy alone.

"Billy? Does your head hurt?" Sandy asked, her hands pressed tightly against either side of his head.

"A little," he groaned.

"Do you remember where you are?"

"Yes, but I wish I didn't."

"Does your neck hurt at all?"

"No," Billy said. Sandy released his head, and he rolled onto his stomach then pushed himself to his knees. "Why's he being such a jerk?"

Sandy was at a loss to explain but tried anyway. "You know how you've never played goalie before?"

"It shows?" Billy asked sarcastically.

Sandy gave him a sympathetic smile. "Well, Sheldon's never coached before. You guys have to work together."

"Gee, I can't wait," Billy said, making his way to his feet with Sandy's help.

"You need to be brave," Sandy said. "Back in the old days, goalies didn't even wear masks on their faces."

"Bet those guys turned out ugly," Billy snorted, putting on his gloves and grabbing his stick. Sandy pulled his facemask over his forehead.

"All right, Billy," Sheldon called out. "Get over here."

Billy rolled his eyes and began to shuffle over.

The rest of the players were crowded around Sheldon, some of them collapsed on the ice.

"Okay, we're going to actually play in a scrimmage, now. It'll give me a chance to decide what position you're going to play. Except for Cody and Billy, everyone drop your sticks. Go find yours when I'm done."

One by one, the kids dropped their sticks into a pile at Sheldon's feet. When the last stick fell, Sheldon leaned down and started throwing sticks to the edges of the ice, alternating between sides. When he was done, there were six sticks on one side of the rink and seven on the other.

The players made their way to the individual piles of sticks to retrieve theirs. Cody looked around. Stan was on his team, but Nicky wasn't. On his side were Andy, Matthew, Michael Samson, who was almost 13, and another kid he didn't know.

Sheldon assigned a position to each player then took up a spot opposite Andy on the left wing. Garry came forward to centre, across from Michael, and Paul held the right. The twins, Teddy and Tyler Cardinal, were positioned on the blueline.

"Everybody ready?" Sheldon asked, moving toward centre ice with a puck in his hand. There were nods all around. Michael and Garry placed their sticks on the misshapen blue faceoff dot. Cody could feel his excitement rising.

Sheldon threw the puck to the ice between the players, where it landed with a hollow clatter. Michael and Garry began whacking at the puck, then Garry lost his balance and fell to the ice, leaving Michael with the puck. He passed it to Stan then dashed forward inside the other team's zone, waiting for Stan to bring in the puck. The moment Stan crossed the blueline, the whistle sounded. Everybody stopped and looked at Sheldon.

"You're offside, dummy," Sheldon yelled at Michael. His patience was wearing thin. "You can't cross the blueline until the puck does. Otherwise you're offside. The referee blows the whistle, and there's a faceoff.

"Okay," Sheldon said, relieving Stan of the puck. "I'm going to shoot the puck into the corner. Let's take it from there."

Sheldon blew the whistle and lofted the puck. What followed had him swearing under his breath. No sooner had the puck hit the ice than 11 players headed straight for it, all converging in the corner. There was a flurry of stick-swinging, as each player tried to get at the puck. Three players fell. Nicky crawled away from the fracas and rolled onto his back, clutching his shin and gritting his teeth. Sheldon blew the whistle repeatedly. Everyone stopped.

"WHAT THE HELL ARE YOU DOING?" he exploded.

No one spoke. Nicky was pulling up his pant leg. A large red welt from where a stick caught him was already rising.

"You think that's how you play? A bunch of idiots chasing the puck everywhere? Don't you guys know anything about positioning? Cycling? Setups? ANYTHING?"

Sandy was shuffling across the ice toward Nicky, frowning.

"They don't have the experience you do, Sheldon," she said. "You're here to teach them." She knelt to look at Nicky's leg then passed him a handful of snow, which he pressed against the wound.

"They can't be taught! They don't know anything!" Sheldon yelled, throwing his stick to the ice.

"All right," Sandy said, assessing the situation. Sheldon was obviously at his wit's end, and the kids were frustrated, too. "Why don't we call it a day? It's been over an hour, and we need to start slow. Sheldon, why don't you go home and put together some plans for Monday's practice? Use some of the stuff you've done at your practices."

Sheldon looked like he was going to say something then grabbed his stick and stormed off the ice. Within minutes he had traded his skates for his shoes and was marching away from the rink.

"What a…" Nicky began.

"Quiet," Sandy warned him. "Sheldon's the best there is, guys. He's just not used to coaching. But he'll get there."

"I hope so," Nicky retorted, standing and testing his leg. "Shouldn't we have shin guards, or something?"

"Yes." Sandy frowned. "We'll have to do something about that." She just didn't know what.

"I've got some time to kill," she said. "Why don't you guys just grab some pucks and have some fun? Pass, shoot, whatever you want."

"Do I have to stay?" Billy hollered from the other end of the ice.

"Only if you want to practice."

"No, thank you!" With a relieved sigh, he tromped toward the bench. "I'd rather practice taking all this stuff off."

Sandy stood at the edge of the rink, watching the boys experiment with hitting the pucks. Sheldon didn't understand just how big a deal this was for these kids, and for the community as a whole.

He'll come around, Sandy thought, but she was nagged by doubt. The hockey team's first practice had been a disaster until the coach left. *That can't be a good sign.*

The crack of a stick on a puck echoed through the air. *Exactly as a hockey practice should be,* she thought. She hoped the next practice was more like it.

"That was stupid," Nicky grumbled, kicking at a chunk of snow in the road.

"Yeah," Cody agreed. He, Nicky and Stan were headed home. After Sheldon left, the players had spent the better part of two hours just goofing around on the ice. It had been a bright spot during an otherwise confusing day.

Cody couldn't understand why Sheldon had treated them like that. Between flurries of weak shots on the empty nets and futile attempts to coax Billy back into goal, almost everyone had traded pot shots about their coach. The only one who hadn't was Cody.

"He's still our coach, though," he said, finally.

"So what?" Nicky said angrily. "Sheldon treats us like a bunch of turds, and you still think he's the greatest player in the world."

Cody shrugged. He didn't have a response. He was definitely disappointed with the practice. And Sheldon...*why would he act like that?* He'd been hoping to learn from him and instead... instead, he'd been ridiculed. And made a defenseman, just because he could skate backwards.

Stan and Nicky waved over their shoulders. Cody watched them until they disappeared from view then turned back to the house. There were no lights on, and the car was gone. His mom was out.

Pushing open the back door, Cody grabbed his stick, then wheeled around and headed back to where he'd come from.

There was no one else at the rink. The sun was already sliding behind the almost endless horizon in a land that seemed perpetually gripped by night in the winter. There was no one else around. The temperature was dropping, and Cody, already chilled, shivered as he laced up his skates.

Stepping onto the ice, he reached into his coat pocket and pulled out a chipped puck bearing the Pittsburgh Penguins' logo—the only valuable thing his father had given him before he skipped out three years ago.

He dropped the puck to the ice, where it landed with a quiet clatter.

If I'm going to be a defenseman, he thought, *I'm going to be the best.*

Chapter Eight

Cody thought school would never end.

He looked at the clock and groaned. He wanted to get back to the rink.

His mother had almost dragged him off the ice Saturday night, and he'd gone back again on Sunday. He wasn't the only one. Teddy and Tyler Cardinal were already there, and Sandy had come by to watch, occasionally offering pointers from rink-side. Stan and Nicky were there, too. Cody had brought along his lone puck, and they'd actually managed to scrimmage a bit. By the end of the day, even Stan, who was probably the worst skater, could skate the length of the ice without falling and was even getting the hang of going backwards.

All Cody could think about was practicing. He wanted to prove to Sheldon just how good he could be. He stole another glance at the clock.

"...Now before you go," his teacher was saying. "I have a message here for the hockey players to meet in the art room."

To Cody's relief, the bell rang. Scurrying out of his seat, he joined Nicky, Stan and Billy, and they made their way to the art room. There, they found Sandy unloading a big box.

"We'll just wait for everyone to get here before we get started," Sandy said, shooing them away from the box.

Most of the players had arrived, when Sheldon walked in. He looked cranky.

"What's going on?" he asked testily. "I'm the coach."

"We have some things to talk about before practice," Sandy said. "You can talk to the players, too. Take a seat."

Sheldon shrugged and dropped into a chair behind her. Sandy gestured to Garry to shut the door.

"All right," Sandy said, as the door hissed shut. "We've got a couple of things to talk about, and I thought it would save time to do it now instead of at practice."

The players nodded.

"Now before I get started, I just wanted to..." Sandy was interrupted by the door opening.

"Is this where the hockey team is meeting?" A girl stood at the door.

"It is," Sandy said. "We'll be done shortly, if you..."

The door swung open, and the girl stepped into the room. She wore skinny jeans, a bright pink sweater and hoop earrings. She was chewing a piece of gum as if she was trying to kill it.

"I'm Samantha Bruno," she said. "I want to play."

There was stunned silence, and then the room erupted.

"Get lost!" Paul jeered. "Go back to playing with your make-up."

"Hey, if she wants to change with us, why not?" Nicky quipped.

"Is a girl even strong enough to play hockey?"

"No way!" Sheldon said, shaking his head. "There ain't gonna be no girls on my team."

"I can skate," Samantha said. "My brothers taught me. And I can shoot, too."

"And I can wear a dress, but you don't see me figure skating," Nicky said. He smirked and nudged Cody in the arm.

But Cody wasn't paying attention. He couldn't keep his eyes off Samantha.

"Quiet!" Sandy shouted. She waited for the hubbub to die down. "Why can't she play?"

"Hello?" Sheldon said. "She's a girl."

"And you don't think girls can play hockey?" Sandy replied. "Ever heard of Hayley Wickenheiser?"

Sheldon promptly closed his mouth. He did know the name. Wickenheiser, from Shaunavon, Saskatchewan, was playing for a men's pro team in Sweden. Stumped for a response, he folded his arms across his chest and shrugged.

Sandy turned to Samantha and smiled. "Welcome to the team, Samantha. Take a seat. I was just going to talk to everyone."

Samantha tossed her hair and strode to a chair in the centre of room. The boys continued to snicker.

"That's enough," Sandy said. "First off, I've got good news." She reached behind her and pulled something out of the box. "You've all got helmets now."

"Whoa!" The snickers turned to murmurs of appreciation.

Sandy had spent the previous night on the phone with Doug, recounting the horrors of the team's first practice. Doug had made a few suggestions, even offering to pay for the helmets.

"That's all the equipment we can afford, right now," Sandy said. "But it's the most important. For shin pads," she added, "we'll have to use those." She pointed to a nearby table stacked with magazines and catalogues. The magazines had been Doug's idea. "A long time ago, that's what kids used to protect their legs. They'd hold them in place with these jar sealer rings." She held one up for inspection. "Everyone grab two of those and handful of these," she said. "It's the best we can do until we can get real pads."

"Got any *Playboy*s?" Sheldon snickered.

Sandy ignored him. "Now, I've also got some other news. We're going to keep practicing with our coach like we did before, but we're also going to be working toward something more than just learning how to play." Sandy paused. "In three weeks, we're going to play a real game against another team."

"You've gotta be kidding!" Sheldon looked sceptical. "They aren't ready to play a kindergarten class."

"Who are we playing?" Stan boomed from the back.

"Peace River," Sandy said. "We're going to play two games, the first one there and the second one here. They're a house league team, not a AAA team or anything."

She had Doug to thank for the games; he'd used his contacts to arrange them. Sandy smiled, remembering his enthusiasm. The more she'd talked to him about the team, the more interested Doug had become.

"So, we're going to get our butts whipped twice?" Billy asked.

"I'm sure if you work hard with your coach, anything is possible."

Sheldon, however, was shaking his head. "We don't have a chance."

"How about a little support?" Sandy hissed over her shoulder. "They could use it."

"They weren't soaking up much of what I was teaching on Saturday," Sheldon retorted. "What do you expect me to do in three weeks?"

Sandy decided to ignore him, for now. "So, everyone, including Samantha, come get a helmet and get fitted. I'll see you at the rink at six tonight."

Chairs scraped against the floor, as the players leapt from their seats and hurried up to the front. Sandy spent the next half hour, screwdriver in hand, making sure every single helmet and face cage fit snugly and securely.

The stack of magazines had been reduced to a small pile when the last players headed out the door. Samantha was the last to leave.

"I can play," she said, turning back.

"Don't tell me, sweetheart." Sandy smiled. "Show them on the ice tonight."

"I think this is a very bad idea," Billy whined.

"Shut up, Chalifoux," Sheldon replied, wrapping strips of fabric around the goaltender's left arm.

Today's practice had been better…barely. Some of the players had gotten the hang of skating, but they still knew nothing about how to actually play the game. Sheldon's throat was hoarse from yelling. These kids could barely skate, and they couldn't pass, couldn't shoot and knew absolutely nothing about positioning. They were pissing him off.

And then there's that girl, Sheldon muttered to himself. Samantha was already on the ice when the rest of the team had trickled in. Unlike most of the others, she could skate, she could pass and she could definitely shoot.

"I played a lot of shinny with my brothers," she'd said, as she fired a wrist shot on net. "I told them they should come. But they're too busy being idiots."

Gus and Greg were members of the Posse. Sheldon had seen them a few times, hanging out at Lou's. They could play hockey—in fact, they were on Sheldon's team in Manning—but neither of them played anymore. He wondered if he'd ever play again, if he followed in Lou's footsteps. Not likely.

"Ow!" Billy howled, as Sheldon pulled hard on a knot in the fabric. Sheldon yanked it again.

"Look," Sheldon said. "If you're not going to stay in the net, I'm going to make you stay here. You're going to learn that all this crap"—Sheldon pointed at Billy's pads—"will actually protect you. You're supposed to use it to stop the puck, not fall down on the ice like a turtle."

"Did you learn this from a movie?" Billy asked, scowling. His nose was running, and he struggled to pull his free arm out of Sheldon's grip so he could wipe it. Sheldon tugged it back, wrapped it with the thick cloth and threaded it between the mesh and crossbar of the net. He tied a large knot then stepped back to admire his handiwork. He'd effectively lashed Billy into place between the posts. In fact, Sheldon *had* gotten the idea from a movie and had come prepared. It was the only way he could think of to get Billy to learn.

"What are you so afraid of, anyway?" he asked, tightening a knot.

Billy grimaced. "What's not to be afraid of?" he said. "You want me to stand here like a target between the puck and the net, and you think these stupid pads will protect me? They didn't when you dinged me in the head the other day."

"You have to learn," Sheldon said.

"Did Sandy say this was okay?" Billy asked stubbornly.

Sheldon grabbed the front of Billy's face cage and yanked him forward.

"Listen, you little punk," he snarled. "I am the coach, not Sandy. You do what I tell you!"

Sheldon released him and skated away, blowing his whistle twice. The players were circled around the net just inside the blueline. Each had three pucks.

"All right," Sheldon said. "Shoot!"

There was a brief pause then a flurry of action. The first volley was hardly noticeable; half the pucks missed the net, a handful didn't make it off the ice, and the only two that soared into the air—Cody's and Samantha's—missed Billy and ended up in the net. Sheldon watched three players, who had fallen while trying to shoot, pick themselves up. He growled in exasperation.

Grabbing one of his pucks, he swung his stick back and fired, nailing Billy in the chest. He ignored Billy's howl of pain as he rocked back and fired again, this one deflecting off Billy's thigh. He fired his last puck, slapping one off Billy's goalie pads, then started working his way down the line, unconsciously pushing his players out of the way and firing their pucks at the net. Each shot elicited another cry of pain, but Sheldon was mentally somewhere else. He was back on the ice in Grande Prairie, showing off his skill to a bunch of coaches who'd just crapped on his dream.

I'll teach you bastards, he raged, firing shot after shot. *I am good enough! I am the best!*

He was reaching back to fire his last shot, when a hand grabbed his stick and pulled it away. He turned angrily to confront whoever dared touch him. It was Sandy.

"What are you doing?!" She was livid. She pointed at the net, where Billy was hanging from the wooden crossbar, sobbing in pain. "Are you insane?"

Sheldon was breathing heavily. He blinked but said nothing.

"Go home, Sheldon," Sandy said. Her voice was hard. "You can come back when you calm down and apologize."

"Screw that," Sheldon said, snatching his stick back. "These kids are useless! I can't teach them a damn thing. And I'm sure as hell not gonna apologize to them!"

Sandy glared at him. "You will if you want to play on this team."

"Keep your stupid team. I quit!" Sheldon kicked a puck out of the way and skated off. Within minutes, he had his skates slung over his shoulder and was stalking off down the road. Sandy headed immediately for Billy, who was still whimpering.

"I'm sorry, Billy," Sandy said. "Are you all right?" She tried to get his mask off, but Billy pulled away. As soon as she untied the last knot, Billy skated away from the net and crumpled into a heap at the far end of the rink.

Sandy sighed and turned to the others. They were staring at her through the cages of their helmets, waiting for her to say something.

"Well," she said, putting on a brave smile. "As long as we're all here, why don't we work on our skating?"

She watched them skate to the far end of the rink and make their way back and forth across the ice. They were getting better, but Sheldon obviously wasn't helping. A pang of doubt ran through her; maybe this wasn't the best idea after all. Maybe this just wasn't going to work.

It has to, she thought.

Chapter Nine

So that's our coach, huh?" Samantha asked. She and Cody had separated from the rest of the pack and were at the other end of the rink, passing the puck back and forth. Samantha had to raise her voice above the sound of the generator powering the two flood lamps lighting the rink.

"Yeah." Cody cushioned the puck on his stick then sent it back to Samantha. "Saturday didn't go so well, either."

"I hear his brother's Posse," Samantha said.

"Yeah." Cody tried not to think about it. He couldn't believe Sheldon would ever do anything that stupid, but he was starting to wonder.

"And he turns 16 in a month, or something."

"We know."

"Just making sure you knew," Samantha said. She stopped the puck with her skate and rested her chin on top of her stick. "You're pretty good."

To his horror, Cody felt his face flush. Samantha's family was new to Watishka Lake; they'd moved to the reserve less than a year ago. He didn't know her very well, not like he knew the other kids on the team. She was a girl, after all, and he wasn't in the habit of hanging out with girls.

Suddenly, he wondered if that might be a mistake. He coughed, to cover his nervousness. "Thanks," he squeaked, using his stick blade to flick an imaginary piece of dirt off the ice.

Across the ice, Billy was wrestling himself out of the goaltending gear. He hurt everywhere—his chest, his arms, his legs. Even his insides ached.

*He's so mean…*Billy thought, pulling his arm and chest protector over his head and throwing it to the ground.

Billy remembered a TV show he'd seen not long ago. Two men at a Washington Capitals game had started arguing about what kind of person would make the best goalie.

"I'd go out and find a big sumo wrestler," one of them had said. "I'd give him a ham sandwich and pay him to stand there. My team would never get scored on."

That's what Billy felt like—a sumo wrestler, pegged as a goalie just because he was fat. He didn't know how to skate, stand or stop a puck. He'd only come out to play because he wanted to make some friends. As the heaviest kid in Watishka Lake, he knew it wouldn't be easy. No one wanted to hang out with the fat kid. *But*, he thought, *maybe if he could play hockey…*

He pulled off his leg pads and yanked the skates off his feet. He felt humiliated. He just wanted to go home and eat until he stopped hurting.

He heard the crunch of boots on snow from behind him.

"You okay?" It was Sandy. He didn't look up. "You can do this, Billy," she said, putting her hand on his shoulder. "You just need some practice."

Billy stood, shrugging off Sandy's arm. Tears welled in his eyes and he sniffed, refusing to let them fall.

"Why bother?" His voice quavered. "I'm just a sumo wrestler." Zipping up his coat, he spun on his heel and walked off through the snow.

Samantha, Cody and the Cardinal brothers were ragging a single puck around, when Cody heard the roar of a car with no muffler. He turned to see it coming across the field, kicking up a gigantic plume of snow as it fishtailed wildly. He could feel the thump of the heavy bass music in his bones.

The car suddenly spun 90 degrees and skidded to a halt at the side of the rink. The rap music, already deafening, got louder as all four doors opened and four men in leather jackets stepped out.

Oh, crap..., Samantha thought, as she saw Gus and Greg exit the rear passenger doors. She didn't know the driver, an overweight man wearing sunglasses, even though it was dark. The fourth Posse member everyone recognized—it was Lou Lambert, wearing his trademark bandana.

"So how's our pro hockey team doing?" Lou said, sauntering over to the ice. He had a big plastic jug in one hand and a smoke between his lips.

No one spoke.

Sandy had turned away from Billy when the car drove up. Sensing danger, she began hurrying back to the others.

"Ready to go home, Sam?" Gus asked his sister with a sneer. "Played with the boys long enough?"

"Get bent, Gus," Samantha retorted. Gus scowled and started toward her, his hand raised. Suddenly, Cody was standing between them, his stick in hand.

"Look at this," Gus said loudly. "A tough guy. You think you can take me, Gladue?"

At that moment, Sandy arrived. "Can I help you, gentlemen?" she asked. She was a little breathless.

"Well, we're running some errands, Ma'am," Lou said with mock seriousness. "First, my buddies here want to make sure their sister gets home safe."

"It doesn't look like she wants to go," Sandy said firmly.

"I don't think that's your decision," Lou said, gesturing with his free hand. Gus reared back and delivered an open-handed slap to the side of Cody's head. There was a collective gasp from the players, as the unexpected blow sent Cody tumbling to the ice. Gus promptly grabbed his sister's arm and started pulling her toward the car.

"Get out of here, or I'll call the cops!" Sandy shouted. She hurried over to Cody to help him up.

"You go right ahead and do that, lady," Lou replied snidely. "But, first, let's get something straight." Lou flicked the butt of his cigarette away and began to unscrew the cap on the jug. "Now, I understand my brother's supposed to be coaching this team. But I saw him, just now, walking home. He was mad. And I don't like it when my brother's mad."

"I thought he should…" Sandy began.

"You thought nothing, you stupid bitch," Lou snarled. "You're not the coach of this team. That ain't your job. Your job is to keep your mouth shut."

Sandy swallowed, suddenly afraid of these men, not because of what they might do to her, but because of what they might do to the kids.

"So here's a reminder of just who's supposed to be in charge. Feel free to have a look at it whenever you start getting mouthy," Lou said with a sneer. He held up the white plastic jug and pulled off the lid.

"I'd stand back," he told Sandy. "This stuff burns."

Sandy ushered the kids away from the rink. With a vicious grin, Lou grabbed the jug by the bottom and began spinning in a circle, sending a shower of clear fluid over the ice. On contact with the fluid, the ice began to hiss, steam and melt. Lou's aim and range weren't great, but they didn't have to be. By the time he'd emptied the jug, half the rink was scarred with basketball-sized pockmarks.

"See ya later," Lou said, tossing the jug the length of the ice. Still grinning, he strolled back to the car, where the others, including Samantha, waited. He slid into the front seat and slammed the door, flipping them the finger as the car roared off down the road.

Sandy stood in shock, as the kids slowly started to take in what had happened. The ice was ruined. Lou had done the worst damage right in the centre of the rink. In some spots, the ice had melted all the way down to the soil below.

Cody rubbed his cheek. It was still stinging. But seeing the ruined ice was what really hurt.

"What are we gonna do now, Sandy?" he asked.

Slowly, Sandy shook her head. "I have no idea," she said.

The old man emerged silently from the brush behind the rink. His eyes, accustomed to the dark, took in the gouged surface of the skating rink.

Curiously, he smiled. He closed his eyes and raised his face to the sky, whispering in Cree for a moment. *Change is coming,* he thought to himself, leaning slightly on his walking stick.

Tonight's events had been auspicious. The ruined ice was proof that the Posse was threatened by the hockey team. Conflict was brewing. It was a battle only the righteous and brave could win. A warrior would rise to the test…just not yet.

He gathered his blanket around him and melted back into the bush. He had work to do.

Sheldon was in bed, trying to sleep. But he couldn't. He was mad. Mad at Lou, mad at Sandy, mad at the team.

It was humiliating, he'd decided. He knew Lou was just sticking up for him, but now Sheldon found himself in an uncomfortable situation. He'd told the team he'd quit, but he hadn't really meant it. He just wanted to play, but he wasn't playing. He was babysitting a bunch of nobodies who didn't know anything about hockey.

Still, it was the best option he had right now. But Lou's behaviour had made it difficult for him to go back. He didn't want to show up with his tail between his legs, begging to be allowed back on the team. He just wanted to play.

He closed his eyes and tried to think about something other than hockey. He couldn't come up with anything.

Chapter Ten

Sandy stared at the miracle before her. She could scarcely believe her eyes.

She'd gone home last night, miserable, depressed, without any idea of what to do next. The ice was ruined, the players were terrified and their coach was, well, no longer their coach.

After talking with Doug, she'd stayed up with Aunty Anne, describing what had happened. Lou and his gang had frightened them badly. Sandy had no idea what to do, except call the police. But Aunty Anne shook her head. Calling the police would be useless. After all, what had the Posse done but melt some ice? Would the police even care?

Sandy was heading off to bed, when her aunt asked her to bring home Billy's mask.

"His mask?"

Aunty Anne had nodded enigmatically. "Just do it, dear."

"Okay." Sandy hadn't pushed it. Exhausted from the day's events, she'd gone to bed, without ideas and without hope.

But now her hope had been restored. Before her was an

impeccable sheet of clear, smooth ice. The gouges and craters that had scarred the playing surface less than 24 hours ago had been erased. Other than a few rough spots—bulges in the ice here and there—there was no sign of the damage that had been done the night before.

The miracle, however, was overshadowed by one enduring fact—they were still without a coach.

"What'll we do without a coach?" Cody asked. He'd just completed several laps of the oversized rink and had barely broken a sweat. That was one good thing about the rink's ridiculous size, Sandy thought: the kids were getting fitter, as well as faster.

"We're going to practice," Sandy decided, silently cursing Sheldon. *Posse be damned*, she thought.

"All right everyone," Sandy called out, walking to the ice. The team assembled around her. "Sheldon won't be able to make it tonight, so I'll run practice."

"You?" Garry said. The players looked at her like she was crazy.

Sandy put her hands on her hips. "I know a little more about hockey than you might think," she said, grinning slyly. "Ever hear of Doug Prefontaine?"

"Wait a minute!" Nicky spoke up. "Doug Prefontaine? The hockey player?"

"That's right," Sandy said. "I met him in university about 10 years ago. Doug was playing for the Oilers then. He taught me a lot about the game, and, though I can't skate or shoot very well, I do know a lot about hockey."

"What happened to him?" Billy asked.

"He got hurt," Sandy said. She sighed and kicked a chunk of snow to the edge of the ice. "Five years ago, during a game against the Calgary Flames."

"The Flames suck," Stan piped up.

"They do," Sandy admitted, laughing. "Doug was a defenseman.

During the game, the Flames iced the puck, and Doug skated out to touch it, to get the whistle for the icing call. But a Flames forward started racing for it, to get the icing waved off. When the two of them got to the end boards, the forward tripped Doug and he slammed into the boards."

Sandy remembered it clearly. She'd been in the stands that night, watching with some of the players' wives and girlfriends. At first, she'd thought Doug was okay. But she'd been wrong.

"Doug fell into the boards with his left foot first," she explained, "and he was going really fast. When he hit, he broke his leg in three places." She pointed to her ankle then at a spot just below her kneecap then to the middle of her thigh. "His leg was practically shattered. They had to put a steel rod in to fix it."

Sandy shrugged her shoulders. "That was it. The doctors told him he'd never be able to play again, and Doug knew they were right."

"That sucks," Matthew said quietly.

"Yeah, it does," Sandy said, taking a deep breath. "But I talk to Doug every night. And he's so proud of what you guys are doing. He's paid for your helmets. He really wants you guys to do your best."

Sandy smiled at her players. Was it her imagination, or did they seem to be standing taller? And was that Billy with his chin up and his chest puffed with pride? *Why not?* she thought. It wasn't every day that an NHL player was on your side.

"Doug explained a lot of the game to me when he was playing," Sandy continued, "and he still does. I don't know everything, but I think I can teach you something."

"Hey, look!" Stan pointed over Sandy's shoulder. It was Sheldon, hiking across the field toward the rink.

"Oh, great," Nicky groaned.

Sheldon was trying to figure out what to say. He was still pissed about the last practice, but he was also embarrassed and humiliated by what his brother had done, and he had a feeling Sandy and the team would fix the blame squarely on him. The only reason he'd come back was to clear his name.

Sheldon dropped his skates on the bench and approached the others.

"Look," he said, awkwardly. "Like, I don't know why Lou did that. I'm sorry about what those jerks did."

The players shuffled uncomfortably. A few of them exchanged glances. Sheldon could read resentment on most of their faces.

He voice took on a defensive edge. "But you should remember that I was asked by the Chief to coach this team. So, you guys need to start listening to me, okay?"

He paused, noticing, for the first time, the ice. His jaw dropped. "What the..." He stared. "How did..."

"We don't know," Sandy said, smiling broadly. "But it definitely helps."

Sheldon stood a moment in silence, taking in the miracle, then seemed to snap out of it.

"All right," he said, all business now, as he started to put on his skates. "We've been working on the basics, but we actually haven't played all that much, so far. So, we're going to split into two teams and just scrimmage." He laced up his second skate. "I'll play, but I'll stop things if I see something wrong, okay?"

The players nodded.

"Okay, everyone line up for a faceoff." He looked around then honed in on Samantha. "Samantha, you'll start on the sidelines and sub in when I tell you."

"Gee," Sam said acidly, "there's a surprise." She dropped onto the bench and scowled.

The group dispersed. Billy plodded off to one of the nets. Nicky took centre ice, facing off against Paul. Cody lined up on the blueline with Tyler.

Sheldon checked to see that everyone was in position then skated to centre ice, where he dropped the puck and took his spot on left wing on Nicky's side.

Nicky and Paul slapped at the puck. Paul fell, and Nicky pulled the puck back to Cody, who began churning his way up ice. He looked up, saw Sheldon open on the wing and passed it to him.

Sheldon took the pass, but didn't return the favour. He danced across the blueline, pushed the puck through Garry's legs, skated around Matthew and fired a wrist shot at the top left-hand corner of the net. Billy hardly even moved. Sheldon slowed to a stop.

"Good pass, Cody," he called as everyone congregated around him. "I think that's a good back-up plan. If you're not sure what to do, pass the puck to me."

"Will you pass it back?" Garry asked, rolling his eyes.

"Shut up, Saddleback. You need to worry more about moving your feet than your mouth. That was one of the oldest tricks in the book I pulled on you."

Sheldon turned to Matthew. "And you need to stay in front of me, no matter what. I shouldn't have just been able to walk around you like that. Get it together."

Matthew didn't respond, but Cody saw his jaw tighten.

"As for you," Sheldon called over his shoulder to Billy, "it's time to man up. I've had enough of this chicken act."

Billy didn't reply.

"Okay, let's go again." Sheldon led the team back to centre ice.

But for the rest of the practice—and the next three to come— it was the Sheldon Lambert show. The other players were improving, and Cody was impressed with how far guys like

Nicky and Stan had come. Their skating had really improved, and Garry's shots were getting harder.

But Sheldon wasn't noticing. He hotdogged it on the ice at every practice, every chance he got. He took the puck away from opponents, skated around everyone on the ice then found new ways of putting the puck past Billy. Worst of all, after each goal, he'd make a point of humiliating every other player around, by telling them bluntly what they had done wrong and calling them names. Billy was at the receiving end of most of the criticism, but Sheldon was also picking on Garry, who always ended up flat on his face when Sheldon stickhandled around him.

By Friday night's practice, it was becoming obvious that the players were getting more than fed up with Sheldon. Two players had already quit the team, and Billy was a hair's breadth away from doing the same. Sandy, watching the practices from the sidelines, had felt a growing "uh-oh" sensation in the pit of her stomach. She'd seen improvement from most of the players over the week, but Sheldon was playing like a one-man team, and the others were growing visibly frustrated with each goal and each dressing-down afterwards. And Samantha, despite her skill, barely got a chance to play.

Today's practice was going no better. Most of the players had grim looks on their faces, and Sandy often heard them muttering curses behind Sheldon's back. Samantha was scowling on the sidelines, and Garry was shooting murderous glances at Sheldon whenever he wasn't looking.

The boiling point came when Sheldon, crossing the blue-line off a pass from Cody, actually lost control of the puck. He chased it into the corner, where Garry was waiting, trying to clear it out. Rather than go for the puck, Sheldon slammed into Garry, driving him into the pile of snow that represented the boards. Garry jumped up, dropped his stick and, before

Sheldon could get the puck, landed a haymaker that connected with Sheldon's left temple.

Stunned, Sheldon fell backwards. But Garry was right on top of him, punching as hard as he could. Sheldon finally brought his stick up and butt-ended Garry in the stomach. Groaning, Garry rolled off Sheldon, who followed up with a slash to the arm.

"You stupid piece of shit! You wanna go?" Sheldon scrambled to his feet. His face was purple with rage, and he was breathing hard. "C'mon, punk! Let's go! Right now!"

But Garry had given up the fight. He lay crunched on the ice, trying to catch his breath.

Suddenly, Stan swooped in, crosschecking Sheldon back onto the ice. Sheldon fell then lashed out with his stick, pulling Stan's feet out from under him. Nicky was right behind Stan, his stick raised, when Sandy reached the fray.

"STOP IT, RIGHT NOW!" she yelled, grabbing Nicky's stick and yanking it from his hands.

"Who else wants some, huh?" Sheldon was back on his feet, waving his stick menacingly.

"That's enough, Sheldon!" Sandy said, her eyes blazing.

"They started it!" Sheldon wiped his lip. There was blood on his glove.

"And you provoked it. You're acting like a jerk!"

"I'm acting like a coach!"

"You're nothing like a coach!" Sandy snapped, turning on him. "These kids have two weeks to get ready for their first hockey game, and you've taught them nothing! They've learned more on their own than they have from you."

"I don't have to listen to you!"

"No, I suppose you don't," Sandy said angrily. "You can send your brothers back here to stick up for you, instead, just like a coward would. You're supposed to teach these kids how to play hockey! Not just do whatever you want."

"I'm the best player on the team!" Sheldon retorted. "You don't stand a chance without me."

"Of course we don't. We need you. But instead of helping the team, you're browbeating them. You need to change your attitude."

"I don't have to put up with this," Sheldon said, skating to the benches. "I'll play in Peace River, but I'm not coming to another practice, if this is the thanks I get."

"You're just going to abandon them?" Sandy asked.

"Lady, in Peace River, they'll need me more than ever," Sheldon called out as he threw his skates over his shoulder. "Until then, they're your problem."

Sandy stared after Sheldon as he stormed off. She was so angry, she was vibrating.

"We're better off," Nicky piped up.

"Yeah," Garry and Stan agreed.

But Sandy wasn't so sure.

Chapter Eleven

unty Anne's herbal tea was usually calming. But Sandy was so keyed up, it was having no effect.

"It sounds like you did the right thing," her aunt said, after Sandy told her about the disastrous practice.

"What choice did I have?" Sandy asked, shrugging. "The team was ready to kill him. I just don't know what we're going to do now."

"What do you mean?"

Sandy took a sip of tea. "We don't have a coach. We've got a game in two weeks, and the team has no one to help them."

"Is it really that bad?"

Sandy frowned. "Forgetting, for the moment, that only two of them know how to skate, shoot and pass, that our goalie refuses to stop a puck and that the kids are wearing magazines for leg pads, they don't know a lot about how to play the game. They're getting better, but it's not happening fast enough."

"What do they need to know?" Aunty Anne asked.

"How to take a faceoff. Where to stand when the play's in either end. The difference between a 1-2-2 forecheck and a 3-2." Sandy ticked them off on her fingers.

"And that's important?" Aunty Anne asked, a faint smile on her lips.

"Absolutely!" Sandy said. "Skills are one thing, but it's just as important to understand the play around you, what's happening in your part of the ice and your role on the team."

"Very much like plants," Aunty Anne said.

"Yeah," Sandy said, nodding. "Almost exactly."

"So the team has no coach. And you feel lost."

Sandy sighed, running her finger around the rim of the tea cup. "I went ahead with this because it excited me, because, after years of being afraid of coming back here, I thought I could help prevent other kids from feeling that way," she said. "Now I've let them down. I promised them a lot, and now we have no coach."

"Why don't you coach?"

"Me?" Sandy looked up. She hadn't even thought of it. "Coach?"

"Why not?" Aunty Anne asked. "You've spent most of your adult life in the company of a professional hockey player. You don't think you've picked up a few things along the way? You're the perfect person to coach them."

Sandy sipped at her tea and mulled it over. It would mean staying longer than planned—*away from Doug*, she thought with a pang. And she'd have to call her boss. But she *could* stay. In fact, she was surprised to find that she wanted to stay.

She'd left the reserve because she'd felt there was no hope of a future here, because she saw nothing but misery, no matter which way she looked. She'd stayed away because nothing had changed. Now, there was a chance to make a change, even if just a small one. It felt right.

"Well…" Sandy grinned. "Okay. Why not?"

"Good!" Aunty Anne smiled and pushed herself out of her chair. "Think I'll go to bed then." She kissed Sandy on the forehead. "Goodnight, dear."

Sandy watched her head for the bedroom. *Aunty Anne is looking very pleased with herself,* she thought.

Cody was unusually quiet, and his friends had noticed.

He, Stan and Nicky were in the schoolyard, waiting for the bell to summon them back to class. They'd found an icy patch, away from the elementary school kids, who were playing on the swings, and from the high school kids, who were smoking in small groups. Stan had produced a puck from his pocket, and they were kicking it around on the ice.

"Weird last night, huh?" Stan said, stopping a kick with his shoe and sliding it back to Nicky. Nicky dribbled a slow one over to Cody, who gave it a half-hearted poke.

"Sheldon's a jerk," Nicky said. "He deserved to get his face bashed in, even if it was by Garry."

"You see where he gets it," Stan said.

"Yup. No Posse for me, man," Nicky said. "If that's what happens, I'd rather take the train ride out of here, know what I mean?"

Cody gave the puck a swift kick, sending it toward Stan. "He's still our coach," he said gloomily.

"Were you there last night?" Nicky asked. "Did you see the way he acted, the way he treated everyone? The way he took off like a *wintakay*? He's a lousy coach."

"No, he isn't," Cody retorted. His hands, jammed in his coat pockets, had balled into fists.

"Yes, he is," Nicky said stubbornly. "What are you, his boyfriend? We all know you're his favourite, just because you know how to play."

"Sheldon's still the best hockey player we've got!" Cody said, his voice rising. "Without him on the team, we don't stand a chance."

"He said he'd play in Peace River," Stan said, trying to calm Cody down.

"We need him," Cody said. "He's good. I just…"

"What?" Nicky asked.

But Cody couldn't say it. He'd watched Sheldon play for years, growing more and more impressed with his skill. Sheldon had scored game-winning goals, hat tricks, power play goals and shorthanded goals. He could skate around an entire team and put the puck anywhere in the net he chose. To him, Sheldon was Sidney Crosby, but real.

He'd wanted to learn from him, but after last night's practice, Cody just felt baffled and sad. The person who came to the ice was not the same person Cody thought he knew. He'd idolized Sheldon, and now he didn't know what to think about him. He felt cheated.

"We don't stand a chance," he muttered.

"We don't even know how to play," Nicky said. "Doesn't matter whether he shows up on the bus or not. We'll never win. We'll just look stupid."

Cody toed the puck with his shoe then kicked it into the snow. Nicky was probably right. How could Sandy produce a miracle in two weeks?

Garry Saddleback knew he was in trouble the moment he heard the school bathroom door open. Bent over the sink, rinsing hair gel off his hands, he distinctly heard more than one pair of feet shuffle in and the door slam shut.

"Hey," a voice sneered. "Tough guy."

Garry turned. It was Lou Lambert and the Bruno brothers—and they didn't look friendly.

"Don't you guys have a Mini-Mart to knock over?" Garry said, scornfully. He tried to look tough, but his insides had gone cold with fear.

Lou grabbed Garry's jacket and slammed him against the bathroom wall. "Think you're funny, too, huh?"

Lou shoved him to the floor. Garry didn't move. He'd had a feeling this might be coming. The Posse, after all, looked out for family. He just hoped that whatever happened to him would be over quickly.

Lou reached into his pocket. There was a snap, and Garry's insides heaved, as Lou held a switchblade in front of his face. Without warning, Lou grasped a handful of Garry's hair and pulled. Garry howled and tried to struggle out of Lou's grip, but Gus and Greg had moved in and were holding him fast. He heard a tearing sound then felt Lou's grip on his hair slacken.

"What are you doing?" Garry gasped. Then he moaned. Long strands of hair—his hair—fell to the floor.

Lou grabbed another clump of hair and slashed again. And again. When he finally let go, the floor was scattered with the long, black strands. Released from Lou's grip, Garry scuttled back against the wall. Lou still held a handful of hair in his hand.

"Touch Sheldon again," Lou snarled, "and it won't just be your hair we cut." He threw the hair into Garry's face and strolled out, followed by the Bruno brothers. Garry heard their cruel laughter as the door shut behind them. He waited until he was sure they were gone then raised shaking hands to his scalp. Except for a few tufts, most of his hair was lying on the bathroom floor. He took a shaky breath, and then, to his surprise, he started to cry.

Outside, in the schoolyard, Cody, Nicky and Stan heard the roar of a car as it approached.

"You guys are next," Lou shouted, as the car sped past. He flipped them the finger, just for good measure.

"Great," Nicky said. His face was pale.

"Next?" Stan asked. "What does that mean?"

"I don't know." Nicky glanced back at the school. "Maybe we should find out. You coming, Cody?"

Cody shook his head. "Nah, you guys go ahead."

Stan and Nicky set off for the school, leaving Cody with his thoughts.

"Bunch of jerks, huh?"

Cody looked up. It was Samantha.

"Yeah," he said, suddenly feeling awkward.

"Living with those guys is a pain," Samantha said. "They're out all night, they never go to school. My parents are about ready to throw them out."

"So why don't they?"

Samantha shrugged. "They still think Gus and Greg can change," she said. "They used to be good guys. They used to be fun," she said wistfully.

"Bummer," Cody said lamely, unsure of what else to say. Samantha was standing very close to him, their shoulders almost touching.

"Can I ask you something?" Samantha asked. "What were you going to do the other night at practice, when my brothers came for me?"

Cody felt himself redden. "I don't know," he said, shrugging. He'd asked himself the same thing and wasn't sure if he was ready for the answer. "I didn't really think about it."

"You stepped right in front of them. They could have hurt you."

"They did," Cody said, rubbing his face where Gus had slapped him. "I guess I didn't want them to hurt you."

Samantha smiled. "Do you think you actually stood a chance?"

Cody gave a short laugh. "Obviously not," he said, ducking his head in embarrassment.

There was a pause, and he glanced up. Samantha was studying him. Her eyes were soft, and she had a small smile on her face. Neither spoke.

Then the bell rang.

"I thought it was sweet," Samantha said. Then she leaned forward and kissed Cody on the cheek.

"See you later!" Grinning broadly, she turned and headed for the school. At the door, she turned back and waved. Cody felt his heart leap and his cheeks flush. A warm feeling flooded his torso, and a smile he couldn't stop spread across his whole face.

"Sheldon!" There was a pounding on his bedroom door and the unmistakable bellow of his father. Sheldon reached for the volume control on his stereo and turned it down.

"What?"

"Your uncle's here. He wants to talk to you."

Uncle Alex?

"Okay."

He stood up to open the door, but his uncle was already there.

"Can we talk?" the Chief said. His face was stern.

Uh, oh, Sheldon thought, tensing.

His uncle tossed a pile of clothes off a chair and sat down.

"You've disappointed me, Sheldon," he said.

"Why?" Sheldon asked, though he knew the answer. He shifted uneasily.

"I spent the morning with Ms. Lafonde. She told me what's been happening at practice." The Chief appraised him coolly. "What do you have to say for yourself?"

Sheldon felt the weight of his uncle's gaze. "Those guys are a bunch of little pricks," he grumbled, squirming a little. "They don't know squat about hockey, and they won't listen to me. Last night, a couple of them actually tried to jump me."

"From what I hear, you deserved it."

Sheldon gaped. "You told me I was the coach," he sputtered. "I was being the coach!"

"And did any of your coaches ever treat you like you've been treating your players?"

Sheldon's mouth snapped shut. He stared at his hands.

"I thought so," the Chief said.

"Whatever."

"You need to change your attitude, young one," the Chief said, rising from the chair. "You need to realize that the entire universe does not revolve around you. You are but one small part of it. You may be a great hockey player, but if you can't be part of a team, if you can't share your skills with others, then your talents are wasted."

Sheldon said nothing.

"Arthur!" The Chief walked to the door and called out. A moment later, Sheldon's father appeared. He looked solemn—and a little ashamed, Sheldon thought. "Sheldon is no longer the coach of the team," the Chief said. "I do, however, expect him on the bus for the game. He will fulfil his obligation to the team."

"I'll make sure of it," Arthur said firmly.

"I expected better of you, Sheldon," Chief Bullchild said solemnly. "Your family, your community expected better."

Without another word, the Chief turned and walked out the door. Arthur followed.

Sheldon slammed the door shut. *Pricks! Why didn't they understand? Why was everyone against him?* Sheldon threw himself back onto the bed. *Hockey was his life. Without it, he was nothing.* Tears stung his eyes, and he brushed them away angrily. He stared up at the ceiling, at the posters of Wayne Gretzky and Paul Lemieux he'd tacked up there when he was just six. He'd wanted so much to be like them.

Sheldon wrestled with his emotions. He was ashamed and angry but not sure who he was angry with. He was starting to realize it might be with himself.

He knew there was only one solution. He'd have to show them on the ice.

Chapter Twelve

ody had no idea why they were here.

Sandy had called the players and told them to meet her at the community hall. Now they were sitting on plastic folding chairs, facing an enormous whiteboard with an overhead sketch of a hockey rink on it. Sandy was standing beside it, clutching a handful of markers.

"All right," she said, once the last of the players had arrived. "First some news. After some discussion, Chief Bullchild and I have decided that Sheldon will continue to play with the team, but that he won't be coaching anymore. I will."

"Thank God," Billy said, looking relieved.

Cody's heart sank. *The team was screwed now*, he thought miserably. Then a hand slipped into his and squeezed. It was Samantha's. He felt a flutter in his chest and his misery lift. With a shy grin, Cody squeezed back.

"We've got less than two weeks until our game in Peace River," Sandy said. "As I said before, these guys aren't future Oilers. They play in a recreational house league. They might have been playing for longer, but that doesn't matter that much. You guys have come a long way in the last week. But we need to work on strategy, now."

She motioned to the whiteboard. "We're going to have what they used to call a 'chalk talk,'" she said. "We're going to talk about what you're supposed to be doing on the ice. Then we'll spend the rest of our practices working on it, along with skating, passing and shooting. Okay?"

The players nodded enthusiastically.

"Okay, you guys know what to do on a faceoff at centre ice. That's good. But knowing where to be in other ends is important, too. Let's start with when the puck is in the other team's end…"

Sandy was helping Billy into his equipment. Billy was usually the last one to arrive at the rink, and Sandy usually had to cajole him onto the ice. Even with Sheldon gone, he was reluctant to play.

"Where's my mask?" Billy asked. Instead of his goaltending mask, Sandy had given him a regular helmet and a neck protector.

"Aunty Anne is doing something special with it," she said. "You'll get it back soon."

It was Friday night, and the team was out on the ice for a last practice before the Peace River game the next afternoon. While Sandy was helping Billy, Father Savard was working with the players on positioning, passing and shooting. Sandy had come up with a comfortable formula for practices over the past two weeks. At Doug's suggestion, the players spent an hour on fundamentals: skating, crossovers, stickhandling, passing and shooting. The next 45 minutes were devoted solely to game play, covering different scenarios based on the chalk talk they'd had the week before. The final 15 minutes were spent scrimmaging, with Sandy patrolling the sidelines, whistling when she noticed a mistake and offering advice on improving the play in different situations, even sketching the play out on the whiteboard.

With each practice, Sandy noticed a visible change in the team. Gone were the head-down, lame-dog expressions they'd adopted when Sheldon was in charge. Every step forward, every new skill mastered served to bolster each player's confidence and his effort on the ice. Even Garry and Paul, who could barely stand up straight on skates three weeks ago, were skating with confidence, pushing the puck as they went and stopping on cue. Passes were getting sharper, and some of the shots had enough snap to them to actually leave the surface of the ice.

The biggest improvement had come from Cody. His skating had improved four-fold—remarkable, she thought, for a kid who already knew how to skate. His head was always up, evaluating the play, and, more often than not, he made the right choice on what to do with the puck. With Sheldon gone, Sandy noticed more and more players gravitating to Cody and trying to emulate him on the ice. Cody, given the naïve, good-natured kid that he was, hadn't noticed. But Sandy had. He had also developed chemistry—both on and off the ice— with Samantha. Off the ice, they were inseparable. On the ice, they seemed to communicate telepathically, instinctively knowing where the other was.

Only one player hadn't made much progress, and that was Billy, who still refused to believe that his equipment would protect him. No matter how much Sandy cajoled, nagged and encouraged him, Billy refused to trust his padding. Every practice ended the same way—Billy would make an effort for the first flurry of shots then flee the net for the remainder of the practice. At times, Sandy had to bite her lip to keep from yelling at him, and she almost—almost—felt she understood Sheldon's frustration.

Despite the team's efforts and improvement, Sandy wondered what tomorrow held for these kids. They were better, but they still weren't good. They had had three weeks' practice, whereas the Peace River players had probably been playing for years. Tonight was a last gasp before what Sandy felt would be a devastating experience, but she at least had to give them the hope that they could actually play.

Tonight, the players had warmed up with skating drills, some tentatively turning circles using crossovers, others practicing their front-to-back transitions. Now, they were working on defensive zone play. Sandy knew she needed to work with Billy. She had to try to bring him around.

"Still scared?" Sandy asked.

Billy nodded. "Who in their right mind does this?"

"Billy, the goalie is the greatest player on any team," Sandy said. "He's the one who's always on the ice, who can affect the play almost any time he wants. It takes a very special person to do it."

"I'm not special," Billy muttered.

"Oh, yes you are, Little Buffalo. You didn't choose to play goal, it chose you."

"Sheldon chose me," Billy retorted, eyes flashing.

Sandy shook her head. "It only seems like he did," she said. "But when we handed out skates at our first practice and your turn came, those goalie skates were the only pair left. It might seem like a fluke, but I think there's more to it than that." Sandy hefted the stick in her hands and skated out aways. "I'll help you. Get in net."

"Just don't hurt me," Billy whined, for what must have been the hundredth time.

For the next 30 minutes, Sandy focused entirely on Billy. She moved slowly at first then faster, from one side of the ice to the next, demanding that Billy follow her in his goal crease. At first he stumbled over his skates, but in time his shuffle became less tentative and more forceful. She emptied a basket of pucks onto the ice and started tossing them at Billy, to give him a feel for the puck. When he seemed more comfortable, Sandy floated soft shots on goal that rebounded off his pads, blocker and catcher. She told him to throw his stick aside then started shooting pucks at all four corners of the net, forcing Billy to move to stop them. More often than not, she scored, but by the end, Billy was getting better. And he didn't seem as fearful.

"Better?" she asked, puffing.

"I guess so," Billy said. "If Sheldon had done that right from the start, it would have helped."

"Sheldon has a lot to learn, too," Sandy replied.

"What do you mean? He's a great hockey player."

Sandy smiled. "That's not what I meant."

It was all Sandy could do not to laugh as she held her cell phone up with the video camera on.

Minutes earlier, she'd called the players to centre ice, promising a break before 10 hard laps around the rink. Instead, she'd blown her whistle. Father Savard, on cue, tossed her an inflatable beach ball, then Sandy divided the players into two teams, blew the whistle and tossed the ball up into the air before retreating to the sidelines. Chaos ensued.

Back and forth the two teams went, throwing, punching and passing the ball with their hands in an effort to score. But no one was counting. Players fell over one another and tackled each other playfully, and even Billy tried to rush the beach ball up the ice to score a goal. It was fun, and that's exactly what Sandy had wanted.

At 8:00 PM, she blew the whistle. The morning would come quickly. She encouraged them to get a good night's sleep and eat a healthy breakfast.

"And I mean more than a Coke and a bag of chips," she said, winking.

As she collected her belongings, Sandy caught sight of Cody and Samantha walking off, their hands intertwined. She smiled, and, with a pang, thought of Doug. She missed him.

He should be here, she thought. *He should see what we've done.*

During the two weeks before the game, Sheldon had been examining his future—up close and personal.

He didn't see the point in going to classes, so he skipped school, giving his parents vague answers about where he was going and what he was doing. He could tell, from the worried looks they gave him, that they had their suspicions, but he didn't care. He'd be out of there soon enough.

Where Sheldon was going, almost every day now, was across the reserve to the trailer park, where Lou always welcomed him with open arms.

Sheldon learned something new about Lou every day, some of it appealing, some not. Although Sheldon spent most of his time at Lou's watching TV and drinking beer, Lou came and went at all hours. People Sheldon didn't recognize—and wouldn't want to meet in a dark alley—appeared regularly at the door. Lou spoke with them in hushed tones, and, after a few moments, they would leave. Though Lou never explained what was going on, Sheldon knew—you didn't have to be a brain surgeon to figure out that drugs were involved.

A couple of times, Sheldon had offered to tag along with Lou, but his brother had just grinned. "Soon," he'd said and sauntered out the door.

So Sheldon sat alone and drank. Lou never seemed to run out of beer and cigarettes. Searching a kitchen drawer one day, for a clean knife to make a sandwich, Sheldon had found several thick wads of cash. Just to see what Lou would say, Sheldon asked him if he had a job. A few Posse members were sitting around, smoking, and they'd all laughed, including Lou.

"Sure, bro," he'd said. We work jobs." We winked at his buddies. "And they pay, man. They pay." Then they'd laughed some more, while Sheldon tried to figure out what was so damn funny.

Sheldon had his suspicions about what Lou was doing, but kept his questions to himself. This Posse was a strange creature, fun from one perspective, terrifying from another. No matter what he saw, Sheldon found himself torn about what his future would be like. For the most part, Lou's Posse friends seemed like fun guys who just hung out, did their "jobs" and never had much to worry about. They always had cash, booze, cars and women around. They didn't have a care in the world, as far as Sheldon could tell.

But Sheldon knew where the cash came from. Though Posse life appeared to be free and easy, Sheldon had learned that most of the gang hanging out at Lou's had been in jail, most of them more than once. They wore their time as a badge of honour, an experience that bolstered their "street cred." Sheldon had never set foot inside prison, not even to visit Lou. He'd listened to their horror stories of fights, beatings and gang battles behind bars. When Sheldon really thought about it, when he looked past all the bravado, it actually seemed pathetic.

On Friday night, Lou had come back from another mysterious outing, with the usual suspects in tow.

"Time to party, little bro," Lou said, handing him a beer. "This is the good life."

Over the next several hours, Sheldon watched the party unfold. By midnight, he'd had enough.

"What do you think?" Lou asked, collapsing on the couch next to him. Lou's eyes were bloodshot, his pupils dilated. He reeked of smoke and could barely string two words together.

This is it? Sheldon wondered. *This is how I could "rule"?*

"I think it's time to go home," Sheldon said, struggling to stand. He'd lost track of how many beers he'd had.

"Something I said?" Lou asked.

"No, just...you know. Mom and Dad. They don't want me here," Sheldon said, pulling on his coat and looking for his shoes.

"This is it, bro," Lou said. "This is the life. Not a care in the world, not a person who doesn't respect you." Lou kept talking as Sheldon tied his sneakers. "I rule this place, man. And some day you could, too."

Sheldon looked at his brother—dressed in an undershirt, covered in tattoos, blood caked in his nostrils. He might rule, Sheldon thought, but, right now, he didn't look like he even knew where "this place" was.

But would that be so bad? Sheldon wondered.

"Gotta go, man," he said. "Got a game tomorrow."

"Right," Lou said, stumbling over for a quick embrace. "Don't worry. We got a plan. No one will mess with you after tonight, I promise."

Sheldon hugged his brother back then let himself out into the frigid, empty darkness. He assumed Lou was talking about his future in the Posse. He couldn't have been more wrong.

Sandy knew what a gunshot sounded like. She'd grown up on a reserve, after all.

The crack split the night, waking her instantly. She heard several more shots and then the sound of breaking glass.

Sandy threw herself on the floor as a bullet crashed through her window. She scrambled along the floor, reached up and hauled open the door then crawled down the hall to Aunty Anne's room. Her aunt was cowering on the floor in the hallway.

"What's happening?" Aunty Anne asked fearfully.

At that moment, another fusillade of bullets crashed into the downstairs windows.

"Take that, bitch!" a male voice shouted. Sandy crawled into the bathroom and dared a peek through one of the broken windows. She saw two men climb into a rusted blue car and the car speed off. Although she couldn't tell who the men were, she saw enough. They wore leather jackets and red bandanas.

"Posse," she whispered.

Chapter Thirteen

Sandy was tired. She'd been up most of the night, dealing with police officers. Many of the neighbours had heard the ruckus and come by to see what was happening and offer help. Early this morning, a convoy of vehicles bearing tool-boxes, lumber and sheets of plywood had arrived. Many of the folks who lived in Watishka Lake were tradesmen, and they held enormous respect for the elders, especially Aunty Anne. By 9:00 AM, the sound of hammering, sawing and drilling was echoing across the reserve.

Sandy was also angry and afraid. Her first instinct had been to miss the game and stay with her aunt, but Aunty Anne wasn't having it.

"If you don't go, the Posse wins," Aunty Anne had told her. "Why else do you think they came here? And, anyway," she said wryly, waving her hand at the small army of neighbours wielding hammers and saws in the front yard, "who'd dare attack me now?"

Sandy had finally given in, albeit reluctantly.

Now, she stood by the door of the school bus that would take them to Peace River. The players were all on board, shouting excitedly and even singing. They were going to be late if they didn't leave soon, but Sandy was still waiting for one player—Sheldon.

She had just about given up on him, when she saw him. He looked pale and was coughing. As he neared the bus, Sandy wrinkled her nose. He reeked of smoke and alcohol.

Sheldon made to walk past Sandy, but she grabbed him by the sleeve and pulled him away from the door, pressing him up against the front of the bus, out of sight of the others.

"What are you doing, lady?" Sheldon asked, dropping his hockey bag. He was about to push back when he saw the fury in Sandy's eyes, and for the first time since they'd met, he felt a tinge of apprehension.

Sandy grabbed the front of Sheldon's jacket, pulling his face to within inches of her own. "You tell your brother and his pack of slime that if they ever, *ever* come near my aunt's house again, I will personally tear them to pieces."

Sheldon swallowed. He had no idea what Sandy was talking about. And he had a feeling he didn't want to.

Sandy released the front of his jacket and stepped back. "Now, get on the bus," she said tersely. Sheldon picked up his bag and climbed up the steps. Inside, he saw that every player on the team was staring at him accusingly.

What did Lou do? he wondered. Determined not to reveal his feelings, Sheldon scowled at them then threw his hockey bag onto a seat near the back and dropped down next to it. He plugged his iPod into his ears and stared out the window. He might have to play with these punks, but he sure as hell didn't have to talk to them.

Half an hour out of Peace River, Sandy got up and walked to the front of the bus. There were a few things she still needed to address.

"Okay, everyone listen up for a second," she said, the sound of her voice quelling the chatter. "Just a couple of things before we get there. First off, we're going to be playing two 20-minute, straight-time periods. That means the clock won't stop at all. It's not a full game, but it's the best we could get for ice time.

"We're playing the Peace River Bullets. Like I said, they're a recreational team, just like us. There's no body checking and no slapshots allowed.

"Now," she said, using her hands to steady herself as the bus lurched down the highway, "we forgot to make one important decision. A name... What are we going to call ourselves?"

"What do you mean?" Teddy asked.

"We need a team name. I know we don't have jerseys, yet, but we still need to be called something. What should it be?"

"How about the Cry Babies," Sheldon quipped.

"That's not helpful, Sheldon," Sandy admonished him. "Anyone else?" She looked around hopefully, but most of the players looked blank.

Cody squirmed briefly then mustered his courage and raised his hand.

"How about the Warriors?" he asked.

Sandy mulled it over. It seemed appropriate, both from a historical point of view and as a reflection of what the team was attempting to do. There was no doubt they were warriors.

"Anyone object?" Sandy asked. Sheldon raised his hand, but Sandy didn't acknowledge him.

"All right then. Watishka Warriors it is!" Sandy beamed as the players gave a cheer. "As soon as one of your parents wins at bingo," she added, "we'll get some jerseys made."

Before long, the bus passed a sign welcoming visitors to Peace River and they were pulling up to the arena.

"Everyone grab your stuff and follow me," Sandy said, as the bus lurched to a stop. There was a crush inside the bus, as players struggled to lift bags, sticks and boxes. Sheldon, shouldering his hockey bag and three sticks, bulldozed his way out the door.

Sandy led the crew into the arena. Awed, the players looked around them, while Sandy checked a nearby whiteboard— *Watishka Lake First Nation, Room 2.*

She motioned to the team and led them down a hallway to the appropriate dressing room.

It was nothing special. The last team to play had left a few balls of sock tape behind, but it was clean. The walls were pockmarked with black scuffmarks, the rubber on the floor creased by hundreds of skate blades. A single red bench wound its way around the circumference of the room.

Sandy glanced at the dressing room clock. They were cutting things close. Game time was less than 30 minutes away.

"Okay, let's get ready. If you need help with your skates, let someone know."

Sandy headed over to help Billy with his equipment, while the team began dressing in their makeshift gear: copies of *Marie Clare* and *Maclean's* strapped around their shins with jar sealer rings under their sweatpants and jeans.

Samantha stood uncomfortably for a moment then grabbed her equipment, walked into a toilet stall and closed the door.

"Everyone take one of these," Sandy said, reaching into a box. She began tossing out black pinnies she'd borrowed from the school. "We all have to be wearing something identical."

What chatter there was in the room evaporated into nervous silence. Samantha emerged from the bathroom, skates and helmet on, and took a seat beside Cody, who was bouncing his knees up and down. The Cardinal brothers were staring at the floor, their foreheads pressed against their sticks. Billy looked as if he was about to cry. Sheldon, the only player on the team wearing a full set of equipment, looked like a football player compared to the others.

"Just remember what we talked about the last few days," Sandy said encouragingly. "Play your positions, and play smart. Do the best you can."

"And if you can't, pass the puck to me," Sheldon said.

Sandy ignored him. She scanned the room, making eye contact with each player. "Remember," she said, "you're warriors. You can do this."

There was a whistle from the hallway outside.

"Okay." Sandy smiled. "Let's go play hockey!"

The Bullets were already on the ice. Billy, who was leading the Warriors out of the dressing room stopped briefly, mesmerized.

All of the players wore matching uniforms with a logo. Even for a recreational team, their movements were crisp, confident and well-practiced.

Billy plodded toward the goal at the far end of the rink, while the rest of the team began skating laps around their half of the ice, warming up themselves before they warmed up Billy.

Standing behind the bench in the Warriors' box, Sandy shifted her gaze from one end of the ice to the other. The two teams were polar opposites. The Bullets, all dressed the same, moved almost in unison, with purpose. Her team, dressed in a mishmash of sweat suits, jeans and jackets, were struggling just to stay organized in the warm-up drills she'd taught them. Sheldon wasn't even participating. He was skating alone in a corner. Sandy knew she'd have to play him a lot, even though he didn't deserve it.

A whistle sounded. The referee came over and shook her hand as the teams collected their pucks.

"They're not much to look at," the ref commented, as he skated away.

Sandy shuddered. No matter how hard she smiled, she knew this was going to be bad. She only hoped it wouldn't be a catastrophe.

The players, save Billy, who was inspecting his net, convened around the bench, awaiting instructions.

"Okay, I want Nicky at centre, Garry on right wing and Sheldon on left wing. Cody and Samantha will start on defence. When you hear me yell 'change,' you get the puck out of our end and come to the bench."

The players nodded and skated out to their positions. The remaining players received their assignments from Sandy and made their way into the box. The ref skated to centre ice, held one hand in the air and looked at both goalies then at the person running the score clock.

Sandy looked at her players, who were crammed together on the bench, suddenly realizing that she hadn't told them anything about where they should stand or how they should even change. As Sandy leaned over to give them a quick tutorial, pointing the defensemen to one end of the bench and the forwards to the other, the referee dropped the puck onto the blue dot at centre ice. The game was on.

Chapter Fourteen

Cody was too surprised to be terrified. Nicky had actually won the faceoff, and the puck was coming right to him.

But as quickly as the puck hit his stick, three Bullets players were rushing at him full bore. Cody trapped the puck and fired it through two Bullets players to Sheldon. Despite Sheldon's behaviour, Cody knew that Sheldon was the team's only hope.

Sheldon took the pass in stride just past the redline and danced into the Bullets' zone. Barrelling in on goal, Sheldon continued stickhandling then rifled a shot at the top corner.

Instead of hitting mesh, the puck clanged off the crossbar. A Bullets defender scooped it up behind the net and fired a quick pass up the boards. Cody swallowed, as a line of players in blue sweaters rushed up the ice. The puck carrier was headed right for him. Cody waited until the last possible moment then flashed his stick out. The move dislodged the puck, sending it skittering into the corner. Cody turned to skate forward, got to the puck first then threw it up the middle of the ice, right in front of his own goalie.

The Bullets were waiting. A player in a black helmet picked off Cody's clearing attempt and, without a pause, snapped a shot on goal. Billy screamed as it caromed off his blocker into the corner. Samantha pounced on the puck and fired it out of the Warriors' end.

"Use the boards, moron!" Sheldon yelled at Cody, as he made his way up ice.

"Change!" Cody heard and bolted for the bench, along with Samantha, Nicky and Garry. The gated opened, but none of the players were sure what to do. The line coming off was trying to force their way in, while the line coming on was trying to get onto the ice.

"Get on first, get on first!" Sandy shouted, but it was too late. The Bullets had already sent one of their players up ice and hit him with a long pass. Sheldon wasn't even trying to get back to help out the defenseman. The Bullets player snapped a shot high to Billy's catcher side. The mesh bulged, and the Bullets player raised his hands in the air.

Sandy changed up the lines, but had to hold one player back. Despite her command, Sheldon hadn't come off the ice.

"Change!" she yelled again, but Sheldon wasn't listening.

The referee led both sides to centre ice and dropped the puck again. This time, the Bullets won the faceoff, dumping the puck deep into the Warriors' zone. Tyler Cardinal, playing defence and still the weakest skater on the team, edged his way around the net to stop the puck. Two Bullets forwards converged on him behind the net, pressing him up against the boards, trying to pry the puck free. One of the Bullets forwards finally pried the puck loose, took two strides to the side and centred the puck. The centreman standing in the slot wasted no time one-timing the puck along the ice. Billy fell to his knees to block the shot but not before the puck slid behind him, landing in the back of the goal with a resounding clank.

The Bullets players cheered again. Just three minutes in, they were already up 2–0.

"Sheldon! Get over here!" Sandy shouted, but Sheldon continued to ignore her. The referee dropped the puck.

There was no conclusive faceoff win. Both Nicky and the Bullets centre tied up their sticks, and the puck trickled away to the left. Sheldon swooped in, scooped it up and, with a surprising burst of speed, cut straight through the two Bullets defensemen. The goalie moved out from his crease to cut down the angle, but Sheldon was too quick. His hands twitched to the forehand side, but he didn't take the shot. The goalie hesitated, and Sheldon pulled the puck to his backhand then deftly flicked the puck into the back of the cage. The Warriors cheered. Nicky skated over to congratulate Sheldon, but he skated away, heading for the bench.

"Do you want me to change now?" he asked Sandy, with a self-satisfied smirk.

"Yes," she said, pointing at the bench. "Sit."

Sheldon shrugged and sat down. "Let's see what happens."

With Sheldon on the bench, Sandy was finally able to send Matthew out for his first shift. He took up his position at centre, with Stan and Paul as wingers. Samantha and Cody stood their ground on defence.

The puck fell, and the Bullets charged down the ice. His eyes sweeping the expanse of the rink, Cody took in everything: where the puck carrier was, where the other players were and who was with him. As the forward approached him, he instinctively leaned toward the net, giving the Bullets forward open space on the outside. As the forward made his way around the net, Cody stopped, letting him go and taking up his position in the slot. Samantha took off, approaching the puck carrier as he circled to the other side. She deftly lifted the forward's stick and stripped him of the puck then turned and looked up ice. Of the three forwards, Matthew was the most open and skating the fastest, so she fired the puck toward him. The puck hopped over Matthew's stick, but he caught up to it and slapped it into the Bullets' end.

What followed was a few minutes of relatively decent hockey. Sandy, watching from the bench, was heartened. The Bullets were obviously more practiced and skilled, but the Warriors were holding up well, doing exactly as Sandy had taught them. Even Billy's confidence was growing, she could see, as he stopped one shot with his stick and another with his catcher. Although the teams spent most of their time in the Warriors' end, Sandy's lines—without Sheldon, who was still seated on the bench—were managing to get the puck across the Bullets' line and even generate a few shots.

With just five minutes left in the first period, however, it all began to come apart. A pass back to Tyler at the point hopped over his stick, and, when he turned to follow it, he tripped. A Bullets forward scooped up the loose puck and bolted in alone. Billy seemed to freeze and merely stood there, waiting for the player to make his move. By the time he did, Billy hadn't so much as budged. The puck trickled past him. 3–1 Bullets.

Sheldon looked over his shoulder. "Go," Sandy responded curtly. Sheldon hopped over the boards and took his spot. As he lined up against the Bullets left-winger, he heard the player mutter something just loudly enough for Sheldon to hear.

"Half-breed."

Before the puck dropped, the Bullets player crumpled to the ice with a two-handed slash across the leg. Sandy watched in disappointment as her best player headed for the penalty box.

Sheldon didn't stay there long. Off the faceoff in the Warriors' end, the defenseman who received the pass from his centreman found a Bullet wide open at the side of the net. He slapped the pass over, and the forward one-timed it on goal. Billy never stood a chance. The score was 4–1 Bullets.

Sheldon came out of the penalty box looking to exact some revenge, but Sandy had already sent Stan to play in his place. Sheldon skated off the ice and slammed the bench door.

"Called me a half-breed!" he snarled.

"I'll deal with it later," Sandy told him tersely. "You just go out there on your next shift and score some goals."

But it was the Bullets scoring goals. Two players took up residence in front of Billy, screening him from the action. When a defenseman rifled a puck on net, Billy didn't even see it until it was in the back of the goal: 5–1 Bullets.

Sheldon hopped over the boards and skated to his spot on left wing for the faceoff. The puck slid to Samantha, who stepped up past the redline and dumped the puck into the corner. Garry was on it instantly, digging in the corner against the Bullets defender then prying it free. He chipped the puck to the other corner, where Sheldon was waiting. Nicky was wide open in front as two Bullets players abandoned him to cover Sheldon. But Sheldon never thought to pass. He tried to stickhandle his way through and lost the puck.

It was a two-on-one, two Bullets roaring down on Cody. He knew exactly what to do—take away the pass. Except that strategy didn't work, Cody realized, if your goaltender couldn't stop the puck. Cody played it perfectly, keeping himself between the puck carrier and the second forward. With no pass available, the Bullet with the puck buried his head and fired a shot on goal. Billy flinched, the puck soaring over his shoulder and into the net.

"Sorry, Cody," Billy muttered.

"It's not you, Billy," Cody replied, as Sandy called for a change. "It's not you."

The rest of the period passed quickly, as the clock continued ticking. Before it was over, the Bullets had buried two more shots in the Warriors' net. Recognizing Sheldon as the best player on the team, the Bullets adjusted their defence, making sure two players were always close by. As a result, the Warriors were able to generate no more than a handful of shots on goal, none of which were threatening. Another Bullets rush was interrupted by the sound of the horn signalling the end of the first period.

"Five minutes," the ref said to Sandy as he skated past.

"Don't we get to go to the dressing room and eat oranges or something?" Nicky asked, breathing hard. In addition to being outgunned, the Warriors were also outmanned. The team had only one extra forward and one extra defenseman; the Bullets were rolling three solid lines.

Sandy motioned to the team to join her around the players' bench. Sheldon held back, picking debris off his stick.

"I know the score looks bad, but you guys are doing really well," Sandy said. "This is the first time you've played a game, and you're doing exactly as we've been practicing. You're playing good defence, getting shots on goal and keeping their forwards away from Billy."

Sandy looked up at the clock—she had 20 seconds left before the start of the second period. She saved her last words for the most important player on the ice.

"Billy, you're doing well," she said. "There's nothing to be afraid of. Remember, just be where the puck is going to end up, and you'll be fine."

"Have you looked at the scoreboard?" Billy grumbled, trying to drink from a water bottle through his face cage.

"Just do your best."

The horn blew, summoning both teams back to the ice for the final 20 minutes of the game. Samantha and Cody took their spots on the blueline, with Garry, Nicky and Sheldon up front.

Off the faceoff, the Bullets dumped the puck deep. Samantha, skating almost effortlessly, scooped it up and came to an abrupt stop behind the net, looking for the best possible play. Before she could decide, Sheldon swooped in, plucked the puck off her stick and barrelled off. Picking up speed as he skated, he blew past the entire Bullets' team and again found himself alone. His first shot smacked off the goalie's pad, but he followed up on the rebound, tapping it over the goaltender's leg and in. The score was now 8–2.

"I was going to pass it," Samantha snapped, scowling at Sheldon.

"So what?" Sheldon said. "I scored, didn't I?"

The rest of the line made their way off, replaced by the second unit. There was a scrum along the boards, as a Bullets forward collided with Matthew while converging on the puck. Matthew struggled to his feet, grimacing in pain. He could hardly lift his arm. As he glided to the bench, the Bullets started passing the puck around at will. Garry had barely taken the ice for his injured teammate when another clunk sounded from the Warriors' net and the Bullets started celebrating.

Sandy ordered a change and went to inspect Matthew's arm and shoulder. He'd have a heck of a bruise, but nothing was broken.

"Magazines didn't do me any good there," Matt said, wincing.

Samantha and Cody went over the boards to relieve the Cardinal brothers and found themselves in the middle of another Bullets passing session. Sheldon refused to engage the defenseman, instead swiping his stick half-heartedly at him. As the defender went to pass to his partner on the blueline, Cody saw the pass coming and leapt forward. His stick intercepted the pass, and suddenly he was boring in on the Bullets' net all alone. Unsure of what to do, Cody stickhandled the puck, waiting for an opening.

Then the goalie edged too far over to one side, and Cody saw a hole open up on the blocker side. He flexed his wrists and fired the puck for the hole. His aim was true, but the goalie was too fast, deflecting the shot harmlessly into the corner.

The Bullets came at them again, and Cody again faced a one-on-one battle with the right-winger. Though he pressured the winger to the outside, the winger kept cutting in toward the net. Cody stabbed at the puck with his stick but missed. The forward tried to cut past Cody and in front of the goal but quickly ran out of room. Cody tried to back off, but the Bullets forward came on, not even trying to avoid a collision, his momentum carrying him straight toward the goal. There was a tremendous crash, as the forward collided with Billy, sending him sprawling to the ice. The whistle blew, and the Bullets player started to haul himself up.

Samantha was furious. No one touched the goaltender and got away with it. She skated in, grabbed the Bullets forward by the jersey and pulled him away from Billy, who still lay crumpled in a heap on the ice. The forward brushed off Samantha's hands, pressed his face cage up against hers and sneered, "Squaw."

Cody heard. White-hot with rage, he dug his skates into the ice and propelled himself as hard as he could into the Bullets player, crosschecking him ferociously and propelling him face-first to the ice. His satisfaction was short-lived, however, as he felt a stick bang off the back of his calf. Cody spun around to confront the player who'd slashed him, but he was too late. Sheldon was already there, pushing the Bullets player back and shouting obscenities in his face.

The referee and linesmen stepped in, separating the two players. The ref pointed at Cody then at the penalty box. Cody skated over, his face burning. His heart sank when he heard the ref speak.

"Crosschecking. Five minutes!"

Cody flung himself onto the bench. The Bullets now had a five-minute power play that would last until Cody's penalty expired.

With Cody in the box, Samantha was forced to play most of the penalty kill with one of the Cardinal brothers. After the first goal, it was clear the defensemen were exhausted. Cody kept an eye on the clock, willing the hands to move faster, but it was no use. The Bullets seemed to score at will, helped by the fact that Billy, shaken by his earlier collision, now seemed even more afraid. By the time the penalty box opened, the Bullets had racked up another four goals, making the score 13-2. As he left the penalty box, Cody looked to the bench for instructions. Sandy motioned for him to stay on the ice then called for Samantha to change.

With only five minutes left in the period, Cody was determined to make the most of his time. He did his best to be everywhere, taking away passing lanes and shooting lanes, firing the puck off the board every chance he got. He even led one rush up the ice, dishing the puck off to Sheldon, who shot it right at the goaltender for an easy save. It wasn't enough, though. The Bullets just kept coming, and Billy had obviously lost any will to play. With 30 seconds left, the Bullets had scored an additional two goals. With the score at 15–2, there was nothing left to do but let the clock run out.

Sheldon, however, had other ideas. He was humiliated not only by his play, but by the play of the entire team. He'd never been on the receiving end of such a lopsided score. As soon as the puck dropped, he turned to face his shadow and, without warning, sucker-punched him right in the face cage. The Bullets players instantly converged on Sheldon, trying to get their hands on him. Cody found himself in the middle of the fray, trying to keep one of the Bullets players back.

"You guys are jerks!" the Bullets player yelled, finally giving up as the linesmen rescued Sheldon from the mayhem and escorted him off the ice.

The buzzer sounded. The referee suggested skipping the handshake, and both coaches agreed. Cody felt near tears as he made his way off the ice, ashamed of his penalty but certain that Samantha would talk to him about it, tell him he'd done the right thing by sticking up for her.

He was wrong. Samantha refused to even look at him.

Chapter Fifteen

What was that penalty about?"

They were back on the bus, and Sandy was fixing Cody with a stern look.

"He called Samantha a squaw," Cody explained, still fuming.

"Okay," Sandy said, rubbing her forehead wearily. "There was a lot of name-calling out there. I'll have to talk to the coach before the next game."

"What's the point?" Billy asked glumly. He was staring out the window, watching the sun set. "We got killed out there."

Sandy sighed but tried her best to stay positive. "It was your first game, guys," she said, encouragingly. "You've only been a team for three weeks. And you scored two goals. You did great!"

"They scored 15," Billy said. There were tear tracks on his cheeks. "I don't see how that's a good thing."

"Guys…" Sandy stalled; no one was listening. Billy had turned back to the window, and the others were staring miserably into their laps.

With an hour's drive ahead and no enthusiasm for delivering another pep talk, Sandy returned to her seat and pulled out her cell phone to call Doug. The home line rang until the voicemail picked up. She left a brief message then tried his cell. It went straight to voicemail.

Odd, Sandy thought, trying again, with the same result. She felt discouraged. More than anything, she wanted to hear Doug's voice.

Cody couldn't stand it anymore. He'd been waiting for Samantha to come over, but she hadn't moved from her seat. He still didn't know why she wouldn't talk to him. She hadn't even glanced in his direction. He crossed the aisle of the bus and sat beside her.

"Samantha, I…"

"Do you think I can't take care of myself?" she snapped, interrupting him. Her face was flushed. "Do you think I need you riding in to my rescue?"

"He called you a squaw! I couldn't let him get away with that."

"I don't need you to fight my battles for me," Samantha flared. "I grew up with two brothers, two Posse brothers, I might add. If some stupid white kid calls me a name, I don't need you coming to my rescue! I might be a girl, but I'm a tough girl. I'm not helpless."

"I didn't want you to get hurt."

"I didn't get hurt," she retorted. "But the team did. You're a good player, and you spent five minutes sitting in the penalty box. What kind of example do you think you're setting?"

Cody was confused. "Why should I be setting an example?

Sheldon's the best player on the team. He's the one everyone looks up to!"

"Well, they don't," Samantha said. "There's nothing to look up to. But you're different. They look up to you!"

Cody was stunned into silence. *To him?* He didn't buy it for a second.

"I was just doing what I thought was right," he said feebly.

"Well, you were wrong!" Samantha turned away and stared pointedly out the window.

Cody retreated to his seat. The bus was slowing down as it neared Watishka Lake, bouncing up the dirt road to the ice rink, where a clutch of cars was waiting for their return. As the bus lurched to a halt, the kids began reaching for their equipment.

Cody was anxious to get off the bus. He just wanted to go home. He pushed his way up the aisle behind Sheldon, who was in front of him as they exited the bus.

"Don't let her talk to you like that," Sheldon said. "Hang with me, and you'll learn to put her in her place."

Already strung tight as a drum, Cody snapped. He dropped his bags and shoved, hard, propelling Sheldon out of the bus and face-first into the snow. Sheldon scrambled to his feet, but Cody was right there. Before Sheldon could push him back, Cody landed a fist on his nose that sent him tumbling to the ground. Cody fell on top of Sheldon and grabbed him by the front of his jacket.

"What's wrong with you?" Sheldon shouted, trying to squirm free.

"What's wrong with you?" Cody shouted in return, pounding Sheldon with his fist. "I looked up to you. I defended you. I even wanted to be like you, but all you've done is act like a total jerk!"

"You're messed up, man!" Sheldon growled.

"No, you are!" Cody raged, yanking Sheldon off the ground and slamming him back down. "You're the one with the talent! You're the one with the chance! You're the one we look up to, and you abandon us, treat us like crap? What did we ever do to you? What did I ever do to you?"

"What are you talking about?" Sheldon was trying to throw Cody off, but Cody held fast.

Cody drew in a shuddering breath and then burst into tears. Seeing his chance, Sheldon scampered out of Cody's grip and pulled himself to his feet. Samantha moved in to put an arm around Cody, but he shrugged her off and stalked off across the field.

The rest of the players had gotten off the bus and were gathered around the door. Sheldon straightened his jacket and was about to pick up his bag, when he noticed their faces and stopped short.

Garry ran his hands through his cropped hair and spoke two words: "Get him!"

Before Sandy and Father Savard could react, the players were running at Sheldon, fists raised. Despite his cockiness, Sheldon knew when the odds were against him. Fearing for his safety for probably the first time in his life, he wheeled and sprinted away, crashing into the bush in a desperate attempt to lose them. It didn't take long. The players had only just reached the brush line, when Father Savard stepped in.

"That's enough!" he hollered. It was the first time they'd ever heard him raise his voice. "Let him go!"

"But he's..." Nicky spluttered. He still had a murderous look on his face.

"Not worth your time!" Father Savard said sternly. "Let him hide in the bush. It's time for all of you to go home."

Reluctantly, the players turned back and started collecting their belongings then made their way home or to their parents' vehicles.

Samantha looked around for Cody, but he was long gone. She wondered if he would ever talk to her again.

Sandy had never been so glad to see Aunty Anne's house—even if most of the windows were boarded up. She was exhausted and wanted nothing more than a bath, a bed and a good cry.

She hardly noticed the rental car in the driveway. Whoever had come to visit Aunty Anne would just have to excuse Sandy's lack of courtesy. She was not fit for company.

"Sandy?" Aunty Anne called, as Sandy opened the door. "Is that you?"

"Yes, Aunty," Sandy replied, pulling off her boots and tossing her coat on a hook.

"We have a visitor," Aunty Anne said coyly.

Sandy groaned inwardly. "Oh, yes?" she said, trying her best to at least sound polite. "Anyone I know?"

"I think you do, actually," Aunty Anne said.

Sandy walked into the living room and stopped dead. "Ohmigod!" she gasped. Then she burst into tears.

It was Doug.

Chapter Sixteen

S heldon was crouched behind a bush, trying to catch his breath. His heart thudded in his chest. They'd be on him any second. He waited for the crash of feet in the underbrush, but it didn't come. He heard only the distant sounds of car doors opening and closing and motors fading into the distance.

He waited a few more minutes, just to be sure it was safe, then rose to his feet.

"Hello, Sheldon," said a voice out of the darkness.

Sheldon turned, startled. He'd thought he was alone. Behind him stood an old Native man. He had a blanket wrapped around him, and Sheldon could make out a walking stick in his hand.

"Who are you?" Sheldon asked shakily. The man had caught him off-guard, frightening him.

"A guide," the man said, beckoning him closer.

Sheldon stood fast. "You know my name?"

"I've been waiting for you."

Despite the darkness, Sheldon thought he could make out a smile on the old man's face. He didn't look like a psychotic killer. But then, you could never tell. "What do you want?" he said. He tried bluffing, "My brother and the Posse know where I am, you know."

The old man's smile broadened. "Now, that's a lie," he said. "But now that you've brought the subject up…" He held out his arm. "Come. I've something to show you. Something you need to see."

Sheldon stalled. He was curious. And something about the man seemed familiar, comforting, even. He was pretty sure the old guy was harmless. But following strangers, even seemingly harmless ones, into the bush was just plain crazy.

"Come, Sheldon," the old man repeated. "You are safe with me. The answers you are looking for are this way."

He turned and walked deeper into the bush. Drawn by curiosity, and despite his misgivings, Sheldon followed.

"Who are you?" Sheldon asked. "Are you some kind of medicine man, or something?"

"I suppose that title would be appropriate," the old man said, striding easily through the knee-deep snow.

Now that he was closer, he could see the old man more clearly. Although his face was scored with lines, Sheldon couldn't tell his age. His long, grey hair had been pulled back into an intricately braided ponytail, and he wore only moccasins on his feet. Sheldon thought he knew everyone in Watishka Lake, but he had never seen this man before.

"Where do you live?" Sheldon asked, as they trudged through the snow. He wondered where they were going. "Are you from around here?"

"You could say that," the old man answered. Sheldon found his reticence maddening.

"Well, what are you doing here?'

"As I said, I am a guide," the old man said. "One of those chosen by Mother Earth to help those who have lost their way."

"What do you mean?" Sheldon asked, annoyed. "I haven't lost my way." He stopped to catch his breath. The old man was moving pretty quickly for someone his age.

"Really?" The old man turned. He looked amused. "And where are you going?" he asked quietly.

Sheldon opened his mouth to speak then promptly shut it. He tried again. "I'm...I'm..." He stalled. Where was he going? The old man waited patiently. "As I thought," he said.

"I have hockey!" Sheldon blurted, though he wasn't even sure if that was true anymore. "I'm a great hockey player."

The old man nodded. "Yes. Yes, you are. And what has that brought you?"

Sheldon couldn't answer.

"Your talent is truly a gift," the man said, as he turned and resumed walking. "But you are wasting it."

"Wasting it?" Sheldon followed after him. "That's crap!"

"Is it? What has it gotten you so far?" the old man asked. "You believed that hockey was your path, that your talent would take you to great heights. It was your dream, Sheldon. Where is this dream now?"

"Some asshole coach in Grande Prairie flushed it down the toilet!" Sheldon said, hotly. "He ruined it for me!" Sheldon felt tears forming. He blinked them back furiously.

"The coach ruined your dream, Sheldon? Or did you?"

Sheldon said nothing.

"What else do you have?" the old man prompted.

Sheldon knew what the old man was hinting at, but he didn't reply.

"What is your dream now, Sheldon? To join your brother? To become Posse? Is that where your future lies?"

Sheldon stumbled and took a moment to regain his footing. "I don't know what my future is," he muttered. The old man had gotten ahead of him, and he had to hurry to catch up.

"Don't you?" The old man paused to let Sheldon catch his breath.

"No. Not anymore. I had a dream, one that would take me away from here, so I'd never have to come back to Watishka Lake again."

"And why does your dream take you away?"

"Because there's nothing here!" Sheldon said, his voice sharp. "It's obvious, isn't it? You can be Posse and be a big man, and if you're not...what is there?"

Sheldon suddenly realized that they'd stopped walking and were on top of the hill that overlooked the train tracks. *Oh, crap*, he thought, seized with a sudden fear. *What are we doing here?*

"A hockey team is like a community," the old man said, gazing out over the valley. "It demands not only personal success, but sharing that success with others. It is a 'team game,' and you must play with the rest of your team, if you want to succeed. The goalie stops the puck, the defenseman tries to protect the goalie and the forwards try to score on the other team. They work together toward the same outcome.

"Your gift for hockey does not exist to ensure your individual success. You must use it to help the team play well. Their success is your success. This same lesson applies to Watishka Lake. Every member of the community has a role to play, to make things better. Don't you think you have a role to play in the community, as well?"

Sheldon shrugged. "I don't know. Maybe," he said, glancing nervously at the tracks. "Whatever. Can we just go, now?"

"Not yet," the old man said. "They will be here soon."

"They?" Sheldon asked, peering anxiously into the bushes around him. *Was he going to get swarmed, now?* But he could see no signs of anyone else.

"Everyone knows this place," Sheldon said, fear squeezing his insides. "It's where kids come to die."

"Yes. It is sad," the old man said. A faint light appeared in the east, and Sheldon thought he heard the sound of the howling train in the distance.

"Are these people coming on the train?" Sheldon asked.

The old man chuckled. "That's one way of putting it."

"What do they want with me?"

"Only to talk. You have nothing to fear."

Without warning, the old man turned his face to the sky and closed his eyes, murmuring softly under his breath. A wind that hadn't been blowing before began to swirl around them, whipping up snow that stung Sheldon's eyes. Through his blurred vision, he could see the approaching train. He looked to the old man, who now had his hands outstretched, the walking stick clasped in one of them. As the train thundered closer, Sheldon was gripped by panic. He wanted to run, but he found his feet were frozen in place.

The old man's murmurs grew in tempo and volume, as he chanted faster and faster. Sheldon put his hands over his ears and squeezed his eyes shut, praying that this would be over soon—and that he would still be alive when it was.

Then, as quickly as the train had approached, it receded into the distance. The old man lowered his hands and his head then opened his eyes. The valley was exactly as it had been before—empty and eerily quiet.

"They are here," the old man pronounced. "Follow me."

He began to descend the hill towards the tracks. Sheldon followed, his skin tingling in terror.

When they reached the bottom of the hill, Sheldon swore he could see something by the side of the train tracks. In fact, he could see several somethings. Faint at first, beacons of white light appeared to grow out of the rail bed, writhing and undulating, yet seemingly fixed to the tracks. First two then three then several more appeared.

"What are those?" Sheldon asked. He was filled with a mixture of fear and curiosity.

"They are spirits," the old man said. "The spirits of those who chose to end their lives here."

"All of them?" Sheldon asked.

"Every one. Many have died on this spot, Sheldon, for exactly the same reasons young Lawrence Arcand did. They had lost hope. They had no one to turn to. Death seemed a better alternative to life."

The old man reached out and touched Sheldon's shoulder. "They will not hurt you. They can't. They only wish to speak to you."

"About what?"

"I'll leave that to them."

The old man gave Sheldon a gentle push toward the nearest spirit. The beacon rolled and quivered.

"Go ahead," the old man said, stepping back.

Sheldon didn't know what to say, so he started with the first question that came to mind.

"What do you want?"

Sheldon swore he could hear a collective moan erupt from the spirits. Instead of words, however, Sheldon began to see images in his mind.

They were horrifying. First, a young boy, collapsed on the railroad tracks as the train approached. Sheldon heard crying, screaming and the squealing of brakes. The scene repeated, the victim, this time, a girl. She was followed by another and then another.

Then the faces began to change. Sheldon moaned. The boy on the tracks was Garry. He heard the squeal of the brakes and the impact of steel against flesh and bone. Now the face changed again, and this time it was Nicky then Stan. The Cardinal twins laid down on the tracks together. And last, Cody.

"Stop!" Sheldon held his hands over his ears, as if to drown out the sound.

There was a flash of white. And then another figure appeared on the tracks—one much more recognizable.

"No!"

It was him. He was older, his face ravaged by hard living. He was wearing a black leather jacket and a red bandana, and his knuckles were tattooed, the letters P-O-S-S-E etched into each finger.

Sheldon heard the roar of the train as it approached. He willed himself to move off the tracks, but his limbs refused to obey him.

"Stop!" he cried. "Please stop. This isn't what I want!" But the train kept coming. Sheldon forced his limbs to move with all the strength he could muster. Then, he threw up his arms and screamed.

Instantly, there was silence.

Sheldon, shaking in terror, slowly opened his eyes. The spirits were gone. There was only snow and the darkness. Every last beacon of light had vanished.

"Do you understand?" the old man asked.

Sheldon was still trembling, but he nodded, afraid of what might come out of his mouth if he opened it.

"What do you understand?"

Sheldon took a deep breath, struggling to put his thoughts into words.

"Those kids," he whispered. "They died because they had nothing. The guys on the hockey team have something—they have the team."

"And what else?" the old man prodded him.

"I have a choice to make," he said realization dawning on him. "I can use my talent to make sure the same thing doesn't happen to them—or to me."

The old man nodded. "Yes," he said, smiling now. "You have a choice to make, Sheldon. In fact, you have many choices. Making amends won't be easy, but at least you understand a part of your purpose, now."

The old man began to walk back up the hill, making no motion for Sheldon to follow.

"And the rest? The rest of my purpose?" Sheldon called out.

"It will reveal itself to you in time," the old man said. "If you knew the whole answer, what fun would life be?" He lifted a hand in farewell and then seemed to fade away.

Sheldon blinked. The old man was gone. Stranger still, he could see only one line of footprints in the snow—his. Suddenly aware of the cold, Sheldon pulled up the hood of his jacket and began to run back up the hill.

His step felt more deliberate, his mind suddenly clear. The anger that had lodged in his soul for so long had been vanquished. Instead of anger, Sheldon now felt purpose.

The walk home was long and cold, but Sheldon hardly felt it. His mind was whirling. He stopped for a moment at the side of the road and looked around at the reserve.

I have choices, Sheldon realized. The old man had been right. For the first time in his life, Sheldon saw himself as one small individual in a giant world, instead of the other way around. He had wanted so badly to leave this place, but he hadn't seen how his leaving could affect so many others. He wasn't just a hockey player trying to follow a dream off the reserve—he was a part of the reserve. And he was a part of the solution. The realization was exhilarating. And it was sobering.

I need to make a change, Sheldon thought, crossing the road. He just didn't know where to start.

A pair of headlights blinded him momentarily. Sheldon held to the shoulder, but the oncoming car honked and pulled over beside him.

"What the hell happened to you?" Lou asked, catching sight of his brother's swollen nose and eye as he leaned out of the passenger-side window.

"Nothing," Sheldon said, with a shrug. Lou was the last person he wanted to talk to right now. He wanted to get home. He had things to work out.

"Get in. I'll drop you close to home."

Sheldon hesitated then climbed into the back seat of the car.

"Did you hear what we did to that bitch's house last night?" Lou asked with a laugh as the car pulled away. "Man, it was awesome."

Sheldon remembered his conversation with Sandy that morning. "What did you do?" he asked, not sure he wanted to hear the answer.

"We redecorated it," Lou said, sharing a smirk and a high-five with the driver. "With bullets." They laughed.

Sheldon was stunned. "Why the hell did you do that?"

"Because they messed with you," Lou replied, as if Sheldon was completely missing the point. "And you don't mess with family. You know that."

"Lou…" Sheldon stalled.

"What?" Lou eyed him curiously. "What's up with you, anyway?"

"Nothing," Sheldon said cautiously. "It's just…well, Sandy was just doing her job. I was being a turd. You didn't need to do that."

Lou frowned. "You're not making sense, bro. But don't worry. You'll understand soon."

"I don't know about that, Lou," Sheldon said. "I'm not…"

"It's not an option," his brother said coldly. "When we come for you, you're in. If you try to back out…well, I would hate to have to hurt you." Lou shrugged, letting the last sentence hang in the air.

The car lurched to a stop. Sheldon's house was just ahead.

"Thanks for the ride," he said opening the door. He couldn't wait to leave Lou and his world behind.

"Remember what I said!" Lou called after him.

Sheldon watched Lou drive off, the euphoria he'd felt earlier draining away.

Now, what do I do? he wondered. *How do I get out of this?*

Chapter Seventeen

T here she goes again," Sandy whispered.

Doug looked over. Aunty Anne was seated in her rocking chair in the living room. Her eyes were closed, her head bowed and she was mumbling to herself.

"That doesn't look good," Doug admitted, running a hand through his greying hair.

"She does it almost every night. One time, she told me not to eavesdrop," Sandy said.

Doug was quiet for a moment. "You know, my Cree is a little rusty, but I swear I just heard the word 'grandfather.'"

"Grandfather?" Sandy looked up then shook her head. "I haven't really been able to make anything out. Besides, that doesn't make sense. My great grandfather died decades ago."

Doug shrugged. "Maybe there's more to it than that."

Sandy didn't want to think about it, right now. She was just happy that Doug was here.

They were curled up on the living room couch, catching up on each other's news. Sandy had spent the last hour telling Doug about the game in Peace River and the ensuing fight at the bus. She was exhausted, and he was a sight for sore eyes.

"So," she said. "What are you doing here, really?"

Doug grinned then studied her thoughtfully. "Well," he said, "this seems important to you. And if it's important to you, it's important to me. So I thought I would come and help. Plus, when you really look at it, the Bahamas are so boring, especially without you."

"Good," Sandy said. "Maybe the kids will listen to you as a coach more than me."

"Sandy, I'm not taking over as coach." Doug shifted himself upright. "You are the best coach for this team."

"But…"

Doug put a finger to her lips to hush her. "You were the best coach I ever had," he said. "You were the one who stayed with me, every step of my career. You were the one who stood beside me when I was recovering from my broken leg. You were the one who showed me the way when I wasn't really sure.

"So, if you're the best coach I've ever had, then you're the best coach for them. These kids need you. I'll help out as much as I can. But you're the one who's going to be in charge."

"But what am I going to do about Sheldon?" Sandy asked.

"We'll worry about Sheldon tomorrow," Doug said, giving her a kiss. "Right now, we need rest. We have a big day ahead."

"We do?" Sandy was baffled. Tomorrow was Sunday. She was looking forward to just being with Doug.

"Yeah. If I'm going to help you out, I'm going to need some skates."

Sandy shook her head. "The sporting goods store in Manning is closed on Sundays."

Doug smiled. "Well, apparently, they're willing to open up for select customers who are willing to drop tons of cash in one day," he said.

"How did you manage that?"

Doug shrugged. "Seems some people out there have actually heard of me."

It was late Sunday evening, but it had been a fruitful day. The players had been summoned early that morning to Aunty Anne's house, where they were divided into cars and driven into Manning. It wasn't until they walked into the sporting goods store that they'd realized what was happening. Doug was buying each player a full set of equipment, from new skates to practice sweaters. The players erupted in cheers, some jumping up and down with glee. Even calm, reserved, hard-to-ruffle Stan was yelling and waving his arms in excitement, until a store clerk asked him to stop because he was knocking over the stacks of boxed skates.

When they were done at the store, Sandy took them all out for pizza before they returned to Aunty Anne's and assembled in the basement.

Sandy was about to speak, when she heard footsteps coming down the stairs. Looking over, she saw Sheldon standing in the doorway. One by one, the players fell silent, waiting to see what would happen.

"Come to quit?" Sandy asked him.

"Can I talk to everyone?" Sheldon asked quietly.

"Depends on what you're going to say."

"Please?" Sheldon asked.

Sandy nodded.

Silence reigned as Sheldon collected his thoughts. He turned to his former teammates and forced himself to meet their cold stares.

"I've been a jerk," he said, finally. "I've treated all of you badly. I've been bad for the team. And I'm sorry." He paused then walked over to Garry.

"Garry, I'm sorry about what happened to your hair," he said. "And I'm sorry about how I treated you on the ice."

Garry nodded, speechless. Sheldon then turned to Samantha and apologized to her. And after her, he went to Matthew. Sheldon made his way through the whole team, apologizing to each individual player. Billy was almost in tears when Sheldon said he was sorry for everything he'd said and done and then gave Billy a rough hug.

"It wasn't right. You didn't deserve all that crap I gave you."

Finally, he turned to Sandy. "Sandy, I'm sorry for everything I've done. I'm sorry I didn't listen. I'm sorry I didn't help. I'm sorry I didn't play as a team member. I don't deserve to play anymore, but if you'll let me, I promise I'll be better. Much better."

Sandy was shocked. *What on earth had happened to cause this?*

"You're forgiven," she said quietly. "But it's not up to me." She turned to the other players and raised her voice. "What do you think everyone? Should we let Sheldon play on the team?"

There were only a few nods. Some of the kids—Cody, Nicky, Samantha and Tyler—simply looked away.

"I'll take that as a conditional yes," Sandy said then turned her attention back to Sheldon. "If you can prove you mean what you say, you can play."

"I'll prove it," Sheldon said, with conviction, seeking out a chair. "I'll prove it to everyone."

"Okay then," Sandy said. Then she called out, "Aunty Anne?"

"Coming dear," a voice called from the bedroom. "Is everything ready?"

"Almost," Sandy replied. She had everyone assemble in a circle in the basement. The new skates and sticks had been placed in a pile in the middle of the circle.

Aunty Anne emerged from the other room, clutching a pack of matches in one hand and a mysterious object in the other. She walked to the centre of the room and held up the object for all to see. It was a braid made up of hundreds of blades of grass.

"Does anyone know what this is?" she asked, receiving in response a series of headshakes.

"This is sweetgrass," Aunty Anne said, passing the braid around. "It is a sacred plant that grows between bodies of saltwater and freshwater. For centuries, in our Native history and tradition, we have regarded sweetgrass as the Hair of Mother Earth. We use it in our ceremonies to cleanse and purify ourselves and the objects around us."

"Do we smoke it?" Garry asked.

"No, we don't," Aunty Anne said, kneeling and holding up the braid. "We burn it and then 'smudge' ourselves with the smoke. We wave it around our eyes, our ears, our hearts and our bodies. We invite positive energy and thoughts into our minds and bodies. With the smoke, we cleanse ourselves of what has come before."

Aunty Anne dropped the braid of sweetgrass into a seashell filled with sage leaves and cedar powder. She struck a match and held it to the gathered herbs; the contents slowly began to smoke. Aunty Anne extinguished the match then produced a feather from her hair and began to fan the smouldering grasses and herbs. The room filled with a sweet smoke.

Then she moved to the centre of the circle and paused next to the equipment. First, she offered the smoke to the Creator then to the east, south, west and north. She held it high, offering it to both Mother Earth and Father Sky. Once she was finished, she used one hand to wipe the smoke across her heart and her mind, around her body and then again across her heart, breathing deeply.

"Creator, please cleanse me of my negativity and fill me with positive energies of love, so that, as I am healed, so may I work for the healing of our Earth Mother," she recited.

Aunty Anne held the shell before each player, starting with Garry. Following her instructions, each of them reached out and, with their hands cupped, as if drinking water from a river, drew the smoke in, smudging the smoke across the heart, mind and body. The last player she approached was Sheldon, who pulled the smoke inward as if he were starving for it.

Finally, Aunty Anne waved the shell over the pile of brand-new skates and sticks. After a few minutes, the contents of the shell burned out. The room was still filled with smoke, but the sacred circle had been established.

For several moments, no one spoke, the participants still held in the ritual's spell.

"All right," Sandy said, breaking it. "Everyone get your new gear together and head over to the rink. It's time for practice."

The players grabbed their skates and sticks, found their hockey bags and tromped like a herd of elephants up the stairs. Billy was the last to shoulder his bag.

"Billy, I have your mask," Aunty Anne said. "Take a seat."

Billy waited, as Aunty Anne left the room and returned with a box.

"Billy, do you know about bravery?" Aunty Anne asked.

"Not really," Billy said.

"In our tradition, bravery is considered one the most honour-able of a tribe's traits. We have symbols to represent that brav-ery, symbols that are also considered sacred by our ancestors."

Aunty Anne reached into the box and pulled out a goalie mask—but not just any goalie mask. Instead of plain white, it had been elaborately painted. The top half was white, the bottom half a shade of cool blue. From the top right-hand corner, flowing to the opposite bottom corner was a painting of a feather. Painted onto the back of the mask was an eagle, soaring high in the sky.

"Wow!" Billy said, awed.

"Do you know what I've done here?" Aunty Anne asked, handing it over.

Billy shook his head, not yet having found his voice. He took the newly painted mask from Aunty Anne and examined it closely.

"In aboriginal culture," Aunty Anne said, "one symbol is considered most sacred. That is the eagle feather. This feather embodies everything we hold dear. It comes to us, because the eagle is revered as the bird that can fly so high, it touches the face of God. Its feathers represent strength and bravery and also loyalty, honesty and compassion. This feather, if you are willing to embrace what it stands for, will protect you on the ice."

"Really?" Billy asked. He stared at the mask with renewed respect.

"Really," Aunty Anne said, patting his hand. "There is nothing to be afraid of anymore, Little Buffalo."

Billy hugged Aunty Anne then placed the mask carefully over his face. He picked up his bag and walked to the door.

"Thank you," he whispered.

Chapter Eighteen

The players took to the ice with renewed enthusiasm, eager to try out their new equipment. Once everyone had warmed up, Sandy started the drills. There was no shooting, no position practice, just skating. The kids had to get used to their new skates and to moving in their new equipment.

Everyone, including Billy and Sheldon, listened closely as Sandy carefully explained each drill. They took turns practicing their crossovers around the faceoff circles. With Doug, they worked on skating backwards. They practiced changing direction, turning sharply and stopping. Despite his protests, Billy was forced to take part as well.

"Every goalie needs to skate," Doug had whispered to him. "It's how they learn balance."

After an hour of skating drills and a quick break, Doug, Sandy and Father Savard split the players into groups by position, working with each unit individually. Nicky, Stan and the other forwards worked on passing. Under Doug's tutelage, Samantha, Cody and the Cardinal brothers practiced their one-on-one coverage, learning how to use their sticks to separate opponents from the puck. They worked on breakout passes and shooting from the point.

At the far end of the rink, Sandy helped Billy. They practiced angles, challenging the shooter and positioning in the net. Eventually, Billy discarded his stick and Sandy started firing shots at him. To her surprise, the trepidation that had gripped Billy for the last three weeks seemed to have evaporated. Now he was attacking the puck, using his skates, pads and gloves to knock each shot away.

The practices continued every night for the rest of the week, and the team was making significant improvement. By Thursday, Sandy was beginning to believe not just in the purpose of the team, but in the team itself. The biggest surprise was Sheldon. He now beat Cody to the rink every day and gave 100 percent to every drill. Although the team was slow to accept him back, Sheldon's attitude had completely changed. He'd lost his arrogance and his penchant for criticism. Instead, he offered constructive ideas. He pulled players aside and showed them what they could be doing better. But most of all, for the first time since Sandy met him, Sheldon played with a smile on his face.

There was a smile on Sandy's face, too, during practices. She felt infused with warmth and affection. With every practice, she became increasingly convinced that she had found something special; she'd found, for the first time, a reason to be in Watishka Lake. It wasn't just the team—it was the kids. They'd come out of their shells, and even Garry had stopped fighting. They practiced hard and talked hockey non-stop. She'd heard from a few parents that some of them were even doing better in school.

Sandy had spent so much of her life studying plants, she'd never really bothered to look at people, especially kids.

Now she watched everything they did in minute detail, wanting more than ever to be a part of the solution on the reserve. She had come to realize that these kids needed protection. They needed her. And, more surprisingly, Sandy realized that she needed them.

The realization also made her sad. She didn't want to leave Doug. But she didn't want to leave Watishka Lake, either.

"Tomorrow we'll take it easy," Sandy said at the end of Thursday night's practice. "We'll need to rest up for the game."

The players gathered on the ice for last-minute instructions before they headed home.

Sandy smiled. "I'm very proud of you guys," she said, speaking from the heart. "I think we're going to give the Bullets a run for their money on Saturday."

The players were just getting off the ice, when Sandy remembered one final announcement. "One last thing," she said. "I believe it's someone's birthday. Let's have a chorus of *Happy Birthday* for Sheldon, who's 16 today."

The players broke into song, surrounding Sheldon and punching him on the shoulder. He was grinning sheepishly. Then they changed out of their skates and drifted off in pairs and threes toward home. Sandy waited to make sure the ice was in good shape, then she and Doug got into the car and drove off.

Sheldon was still out on the rink, practicing his wrist shot. He was about to fire a shot into the top corner, when he was interrupted by the sound of a horn. Sheldon looked up to see a familiar car rolling up to the rink.

He cursed under his breath. He hadn't seen Lou since the night after the Peace River game. He'd almost forgotten their encounter and was hoping he could avoid having to deal with his brother.

Lou got out of the car and strolled over. "Congratulations, bro," he said, embracing him. "You're 16."

"Thanks, Lou," Sheldon said, returning the hug tentatively. His stomach was doing flip-flops.

"Get in the car," Lou muttered in his ear.

"Why?"

"It's your birthday, bro. We've got some celebrating to do." Lou's voice had lost some of its warmth. "Now, get in the car. Let's go."

Sheldon was about to protest then remembered Lou's ominous warning. Reluctantly, his fear growing, he traded his skates for shoes and slid into the back seat of the car. The fat guy was driving again.

"Go," Lou said to the driver. The car lurched backwards onto the road.

"What's up?" Sheldon asked.

"Your initiation," Lou said, peering over his headrest to look Sheldon in the eye. "There's something we need you to do, to show us you're ready for this. I'll do it first, to make sure you get the idea. Then it'll be up to you. Don't embarrass me," he added.

Sheldon shifted uneasily. He thought about jumping out of the car. "What are we going to do?" he asked.

"You'll see." Lou turned away.

Back at the trailer park, the driver guided the car into a garage then climbed into the front seat of an Olds. At Lou's instruction, Sheldon got into the back. He watched Lou take a license plate from a nearby shelf and affix it to the back of the car. Then Lou grabbed a sports bag from behind a stack of wood and joined the driver in the front seat. Within a few moments, they were back on the road, heading for Manning.

"What are we doing?" Sheldon asked, though he had an idea. This was it, the initiation that every Posse member had to go through, but he didn't really know what was involved. Sheldon had a feeling it wasn't something he was going to enjoy. He just hoped he could get out of it somehow.

"We're taking back," Lou said. "We're taking back from the white establishment that took so much from us."

"By doing what?"

"You'll see," Lou said. He was fiddling with something in the front seat. Sheldon couldn't see anything but could hear a series of mechanical snaps. "We're soldiers in a war, bro," he said, fiercely. "We're on a mission against the enemy."

Lou's cryptic remarks terrified Sheldon, but he kept his mouth shut. *If I just lie low,* he thought, *maybe I can get this over with.*

As they reached the Manning town limits, Lou threw back the hood of his jacket and pulled a black mask over his face. Then he turned to Sheldon, who went ice-cold with fear. All he could see were his brother's eyes. But that wasn't what frightened him—Lou was holding a shotgun.

"Pay attention, 'cause you're next," Lou said. Suddenly, the driver swerved the car off the highway and into a gas station, pulling up in front of the door.

"For the Posse," he and the driver said together. Then Lou was out of the car and running into the station.

Sheldon wanted to vomit. Dumbstruck, he watched through the window as Lou approached the till and pointed the shotgun at the young cashier. He saw the woman start to shake and cry then turn to the cash register. Her hands fumbled as she opened it and handed Lou the cash tray. He gestured with the shotgun, and the woman pulled a box from underneath the till and started filling it with cartons of cigarettes. Sobbing uncontrollably, she handed the box over then, at a command from Lou, sank to the floor, out of sight. Lou placed the cash tray in the box and backed to the door, his gun trained on the till. When he was through, he spun around and jumped back into the car. The driver hit the gas, and the Olds roared off.

"I never get tired of that!" Lou crowed, pulling off his mask and passing the box of money and cigarettes to Sheldon in the back. Sheldon pushed it into the empty seat beside him. He knew now what Lou wanted him to do.

"How long did you give her?" the driver asked.

"I was feeling nice tonight," Lou said. "Told her to count to 50 before she called the cops. That should give us enough time."

Lou turned to Sheldon. "Your turn," he said with a grin. He passed back the mask then the shotgun. The steel of the firearm felt cold in Sheldon's hands. He started to shake.

"You go in fast, you ask for the tray and smokes then you tell them to get on the floor and count to 50 or 100, or something like that, before calling the cops or you'll come back and kill them," Lou explained. "Got it?"

Sheldon couldn't tear his eyes off the gun. His emotions rose and fell like a rollercoaster. He'd known, even before Lou had handed it to him, that this was not in his future. Lou was a part of the problem, the cancer that leached the strength from the community, the reason no one in Watishka Lake wanted to stay and why those who did lived such pathetic lives.

He remembered the vision he'd experienced beside the train tracks, the sight of himself—older, worn-out and tattooed—falling over on the tracks, waiting for the train to come. Sheldon wondered if the future he'd seen was for real. *Was it unalterable? Could he still change it?*

You have a choice to make, Sheldon. The old man's words echoed in his mind. *You have many choices. Making amends won't be easy, but at least you understand a part of your purpose now.*

This was one of those choices, he realized. And the right one was crystal clear, regardless of what Lou said. Mustering all of his nerve, Sheldon rolled down the window and, before his brother could react, threw the shotgun out of the car.

Chapter Nineteen

hat the hell did you just do?" Lou screamed. The driver brought the Olds to a screeching halt.

"I won't do it, Lou," Sheldon said, shaking his head back and forth. "I won't be like you."

"Get out there and get that gun!"

"No," Sheldon repeated. He was breathing hard, and his hands were shaking. "I don't want this. I don't want your life. It's wrong."

Swearing violently, Lou threw open his door and ran back, retrieving the gun from the side of the road. He wrenched Sheldon's door open, grabbed him by the hair and dragged him away from the car.

"You have five seconds to get back in that car and do what you're told," Lou snarled, aiming the shotgun at him. Sheldon was so scared that he wet his pants. It would be so easy to give in, he thought, but he knew deep down that he couldn't do it.

Lou reached the count of five. The shotgun started to shake in his hands. Sheldon closed his eyes, whimpering, waiting for the blast.

Lou swore loudly and threw the gun to the ground. "You're lucky you're my brother," he snarled. "But you're still going to pay!"

The first punch connected with Sheldon's right eye and sent him spinning to the ground. Lou started to kick him, boots pounding against his stomach, kidneys and ribs. Sheldon cried out in pain, but his cries only seemed to make Lou kick harder. Just when he thought he was about to pass out, Lou stopped kicking. He bent down, grabbed Sheldon by the hair and pulled his head up, so their eyes met.

"If you tell anyone about what happened tonight, I'll kill you," Lou said. "As far as I'm concerned, we're not brothers anymore."

Sheldon scowled through blood-soaked lips. "That makes two of us," he mumbled.

Lou threw Sheldon to the ground, snatched up the shotgun and climbed back into the car. He slammed the door, and the car roared off.

Sheldon counted to 50 then slowly pushed himself upright and began to inspect the damage. His entire body hurt, and his right eye was almost swollen shut. He tried to take a breath but instead launched into an agonizing coughing spasm. Finally, he pulled himself to his feet and started limping down the road.

He hadn't gone far when he saw flashes of red, blue and white coming toward him. Sheldon looked away as the RCMP cruiser pulled up, the lights hurting his eyes. A moment later, an officer was stepping out of the car. The officer got to Sheldon just as he started to collapse.

"What happened, son?"

"My brother…" Sheldon managed.

"Okay, we're gonna get you checked out. Is there anyone you want us to call for you?"

Sheldon could think of only one person. He managed to form the name on his lips and whisper it before the world went black.

When Sheldon awoke, the first thing he realized was that he was in tremendous pain. It even hurt to breathe. There was also a hand holding his. He turned his head to see who it was. Sandy Lafonde was sitting beside his hospital bed.

"You came," Sheldon murmured.

"Of course," Sandy said. "Looks like you got worked over pretty good." She offered him a cup with a straw. He took it and gulped thirstily.

"There's a police officer outside," she said. "He wants to ask you about what happened. Do you want to talk to him?"

Lou's warning echoed in his mind, but Sheldon didn't care. He nodded. Sandy motioned to the officer, who came over and placed a tape recorder by the bed then pulled out a notebook and pen. After an hour, the officer pressed the stop button.

"Did you know that your brother is head of the local Posse chapter?" he asked. Sheldon shook his head.

"With this, we can put him away for a while. If you'll testify in court. Will you do it?"

Sheldon didn't need to think about it. "Yes," said firmly. He felt no sympathy for his brother. In fact, Sheldon realized he wanted to be in the courtroom when Lou was dragged away in handcuffs.

At that moment, a doctor came in, flipping through a chart. "You're a lucky man, Mr. Lambert," the doctor said, adjusting her glasses. "Nothing broken, no signs of a concussion. The swelling in your eye should go down over the next couple of days—just keep some ice on it and come back if you have any vision problems. I'll give you something for the pain, and you can go."

"Thanks." Sheldon sighed in relief. He started to get up then realized he was wearing nothing but a hospital gown.

"I'll be in the hall," Sandy said hastily. "Doug is waiting in the car."

A short while later, Doug was helping Sheldon inside the front door of his house.

"What happened?" His father paled as he saw Sheldon's face.

"Lou," Sheldon said. "I turned 16 today."

Arthur's face darkened.

"I said no," Sheldon said.

Arthur gaped then pulled Sheldon close.

"Ouch!" Sheldon complained.

"I'm so proud of you, son!"

Sandy helped him onto the couch and pulled a blanket over him. He heard her say something, but it sounded far away. The pain medication was making him woozy. He laid his head against the pillow and closed his eyes.

I just hope I can play, he thought, as he drifted off to sleep.

Chapter Twenty

t was early, but Cody had been awake for more than an hour.

It was game day.

He was sitting in his bedroom, taping his stick, sporting the newest gift from Doug. The jersey was crisp and white, with black shoulders and maroon lettering across the front. It read "Warriors." On the back was Cody's last name and the number 4.

"Bobby Orr's number," Doug had said, handing it to him during a team gathering at Aunty Anne's house following a light skate and practice the night before. "The best there ever was."

Each player had received a jersey, even Sheldon, though he wasn't moving very fast. The swelling in his eye had gone down, but his body was still bruised and battered. And the pills the doctor gave him made him drowsy. He'd been insistent, however, that he would play on Saturday.

Cody's jersey was different from the others. A large maroon "C" had been sewn onto the upper left shoulder. Sheldon and Nicky's jerseys each sported an "A."

"You were meant to be the captain," Sandy had told him.

Cody thought Sheldon should have been the captain. He was still finding it hard to believe what Sheldon had done. He'd said no to the Posse then had his own brother arrested. That took guts.

He had a good feeling about today. The team had looked so good the previous night that Cody wanted to keep playing. But Sandy and Doug had been firm: they needed to rest. The conditions were promising, as well. The weather forecaster had predicted clear blue skies, bright sunshine and a daytime high of −20°C. Cody chuckled when he heard.

Cody looked closely at his stick, the replica Sidney Crosby autograph catching his eye. He grabbed a black marker from his desk, blacked out the name then wrote a different name on the other side.

Doug Prefontaine, the stick now read. He'd have to ask Doug to sign it after the game.

The warm-up was over. It was time to play.

The outdoor rink had changed during the past week. Two sheets of plywood had been braced behind the nets to keep shots in play. Samantha's father, Marvin, had used some scrap lumber to build a row of bleachers, which were now filled with cheering parents, relatives and other supporters from the reserve. Each team had a steel barrel with a fire burning inside—the only source of heat for the next 40-plus minutes.

Because there was no scoreboard or clock, Chief Bullchild was seated at a table between the two teams. He would yell out the time in one-minute increments until the final minute, when he would announce the time every five seconds then every second for the last ten. He would use an air horn to signal the end of a period. In place of a penalty box, two chairs had been placed at the side of the rink, in front of the bleachers.

"Okay, everyone gather in," Sandy called out. The team huddled around her.

"I was watching the Bullets during the warm-up," she said. "First, they're miserable, thanks to the cold."

Everyone laughed.

"Second, they were taking it easy. They think this is going to be another cakewalk. They're not ready for this game. We are."

The team cheered.

"Remember, we are warriors, protecting our homeland. No one can take that away from us."

The team cheered again. Then Nicky, Garry and Sheldon took to the ice as forwards, with Samantha and Cody on defense.

Everyone was surprised that Sheldon was playing, but no one had been able to talk him out of it. Not only was he playing, but he also was playing without painkillers. They made him too tired, he said. He wanted to be fully alert for the game.

The Bullets' starting line skated into place. *Sandy was right*, Cody thought—they looked miserable. Unprepared for the cold temperatures, the Bullets players were suffering, their ears already red from the cold. Their noses were running, and they blinked constantly in the freezing wind.

The referee, used to reffing games in Manning, was wearing three sweaters under his striped uniform, as were his two linesmen. He held his hand in the air to each goalie then to the timekeeper's bench.

Cody placed his stick on the ice and waited. He felt no nerves, no overwhelming excitement. His insides were cool and steel-like, his focus honed to a knife's edge. He was ready to play.

"I've got your back," he heard Samantha whisper. He nodded in response. He wanted to win.

The puck hit the ice, and the game was on. Nicky lifted the Bullets centre's stick and kicked the puck back to Samantha, who skated up the ice. When she reached the blueline, she dumped the puck behind the goal, rebounding it off the board. Garry, Nicky and Sheldon streaked in, as the Bullets defenders lazily skated back. Garry got to the puck first, wheeled back toward the blueline and fired a pass out in front. Nicky one-timed the puck with a wrist shot that bounced off the goalie's pads. The rebound came straight to Sheldon, who poked an off-balance shot on net. The goalie dove and knocked it aside with his stick. Sheldon followed up on the puck, swooping away from his check and dishing the puck back to Cody at the point. Cody passed it back to Sheldon, who passed it back to Cody. He saw a hole in the clutch of players gathered in front and snapped a shot on goal. The Bullets goalie, having just gotten to his feet, snared it in his trapper and held on. The whistle blew.

"Nineteen minutes remaining." Chief Bullchild's voice echoed over the megaphone. There was a laugh from the bleachers.

"Great shift!" Sandy clapped her players on the back as she changed lines. This time, Paul won the draw, pulling the puck straight back to Teddy Cardinal, who quickly dished it off to Tyler. Tyler rifled a shot on goal that just missed the low corner. The Bullets players fought off Stan and Matthew and skated out, passing the puck back and forth as they approached the blueline. But the Peace River team wasn't used to playing on such a large rink. The practiced timing of their passing play ended up forcing them offside.

Both sides changed, and the Bullets won the draw. The left defenseman crossed the blueline and fired a wrist shot on goal. With a calm that surprised everyone, Billy used his stick to direct the puck into the corner. Cody scooped it up, wheeled and saw Nicky breaking up ice. He lifted the puck into the air, watching as it landed one-foot in front of his friend. In alone, Nicky faked a shot to the left then pulled it to his backhand and slid it toward the goal. The Bullets goalie followed him all the way but didn't squeeze his legs together in time. The puck trickled through the gap and into the net. The referee blew the whistle and pointed at the goal. Nicky threw his hands up in the air then accepted embraces from Sheldon, Garry and Cody. The small crowd in the bleachers went berserk.

"Nice pass," Nicky said to Cody.

"Nice shot," Cody answered, patting Nicky on the rear with his stick.

The goal seemed to rattle the Bullets, who were tiring quickly, their legs unused to skating on such a large rink. The Warriors, who'd spent every practice skating end to end, were in prime shape and were actually dominating the play. Both Warriors lines ran the Bullets in circles, with crisp passing and hard skating.

The Bullets goalie kicked out a shot from in close, blocked a point shot then fell to his knees to stop the rebound. By the time the 10-minute mark was called, the Warriors had fired 13 shots on goal, compared to one for Peace River.

"Keep pushing," Sandy said, as she changed lines, subbing Michael in for Nicky to give him a rest. "No goalie can stop shots like that forever."

As if on cue, Matthew won the faceoff in the Bullets' end and threw the puck back to Cody. Just as Cody dished the puck to Samantha, Matthew dug his skates in and headed for the front of the net. Samantha's wrist shot was waist-high, but Matthew held his stick up and used the blade to deflect the shot down. It bounced off the ice and into the net behind the Bullets' goalie. The crowd jumped to their feet, cheering, shouting and banging drums. The Warriors now had a 2–0 lead.

The Bullets couldn't seem to get their game together. Between shifts, the players huddled around the barrel fire, holding their gloves out to warm their hands. The Warriors players, knowing that the best way to stay warm was to stay in the cold and let the body get used to it, ignored theirs.

With eight minutes left in the first period, a Bullets defender knocked Stan down in the corner and stripped the puck away, throwing it up the middle of the ice. A forward caught the puck in stride and bore down on Billy all alone. His newly painted mask flashing in the sunlight, Billy erupted from his net to take away the shooter's angle then started working his way back into the net as the forward got closer. The forward tried a fake, but Billy didn't bite. He followed the player the entire way, stretching out his right leg to stop the shot. The Bullet grabbed his own rebound and threw it out front, where another Bullet had taken up position. As the puck came out front, Billy exploded off his post towards the shooter. The low shot bounced off Billy's pads. Billy slapped his catcher down on the rebound, to get a whistle.

Buoyed by their recent rush, the Bullets started working the puck around the Warriors' end, but the Warriors moved with them, taking away their passes and shots. Then Nicky's skate caught in a rut, as he was crossing to cover his defenseman, and he fell, leaving his check all alone. The defenseman fired a shot on goal. Billy kicked it aside, but the rebound went straight to a Bullets forward. Billy leapt to the far side to cover the empty net, but it was too late. The whistle blew, and the score became 2–1.

"You want some more of that?" the forward yelled at Billy.

"Bring it, chump," Billy replied with a smile.

And they did, but Billy was ready for them. In the last five minutes of the period, Little Buffalo played larger than life, kicking aside seven more shots. In a play that closely mimicked one the Bullets had scored on, Billy stopped a shot out front then leapt across and snagged the rebound out of the air, just as it seemed the Bullets were going to tie the score. Billy held his catcher high in the air for all to see. The crowd loved it. Then the buzzer sounded, and the teams returned to their benches. The Bullets players huddled around the barrel, trying to get warm.

"Wusses," Nicky jeered.

"You guys are playing so well," Sandy said, with a huge smile. "I honestly can't think of anything to say."

"I can," Sheldon said. He'd taken a couple of shifts off; the pain in his ribs and stomach was simply too much. "This is our house, guys. This is our house! And no one beats us at our house!"

"YEAH!" the players cheered in unison. The referee blew his whistle, and they returned to the ice for the second and final period.

"Having fun?" Sheldon whispered to the Bullet player next to him.

"Shove it, half-breed," the winger growled.

"Just you watch," Sheldon said, deciding to respond with his play instead of his stick.

Off the draw, the puck skittered over to Sheldon. He poked it through the winger's legs then darted towards the Bullets' goal. He stickhandled around one defender but let the other remain in front of him. At the right moment, Sheldon blasted the puck through the defenseman's legs, using him as a screen. The goalie didn't see the shot until it was already in the top corner of the net.

Sheldon traded high-fives with his teammates then skated back to the bench, passing the winger.

"Did you see where I shoved it?" Sheldon asked. The Bullets player responded with a two-handed slash to Sheldon's ankle.

The ref blew the whistle and sent the Bullets player to the penalty box.

The Warriors, however, were unable to capitalize on the power play, despite several good shots on net. The Bullets goaltender was breathing hard as he scrambled from side to side, keeping the Warriors at bay. With five seconds left in the penalty, Billy started slapping his stick on the ice to let his teammates know the penalty was almost over, but no one was listening. Just as the Bullets cleared the puck out of their end, the penalized winger erupted from his seat and picked up the pass. Instead of deking, like the last Bullet had, he skated in on goal, stickhandling all the way then fired a rocket over Billy's shoulder. There was a groan from the benches as the chicken wire rang and the whistle blew. The score was now 3–2.

Sheldon tried to restore the two-goal lead with a nice pass across the crease on the next play, but Matthew fired it wide of the goal. As the play turned back up ice, Sheldon skated for the bench and collapsed on the ground. The pain in his ribs was intense. It even hurt to breathe.

"Do you need anything?" Doug asked.

"Just a break," Sheldon said. "I'll be all right."

Doug helped him to his feet. "I can't decide if you're really tough or just crazy."

On the ice, the Cardinal brothers had run into trouble. The Bullets had trapped the puck behind the Warriors' net, a single player stickhandling from side-to-side. Teddy and Tyler held out as long as they could, remembering Sandy's lesson that no one can score from the back of the net, but it was too much. Teddy finally broke and left his post, trying to flush the Bullets player out. As Teddy skated forward, the Peace River forward fired a pass right through Teddy's skates to the player Teddy had been covering. Billy didn't have a chance. Tie game.

"Five minutes left," Chief Bullchild called out.

"Time!" Sandy shouted to the ref.

"The clock won't stop," the ref replied.

"That's fine," Sandy said. She just wanted to rest her players and let the Bullets "cool off." Both teams, engaged in such a fierce battle, were depleted and running on fumes.

"You guys know what?" Sandy asked, as they gathered around the bench. "You won't lose this game."

"She's right," Doug said, stepping forward. "I've been watching and playing all my life. You have them on the ropes. These guys are yours. Go get them."

Refreshed, Sheldon, Nicky, Garry, Samantha and Cody returned to the ice.

Not far away, hidden by the brush, the old man watched with a knowing smile.

Chapter Twenty-One

Three minutes," the Chief announced. The teams met at centre and play resumed.

The Bullets won the draw and steamed into the Warriors' end. The forward dropped the puck for a defenseman, who stopped, then started skating across the ice, looking for a shot. Not seeing one, he passed the puck back to the winger, who took it deeper into the corner then chipped it around to the left-hand side.

"Two minutes."

The forward centred the puck. The centreman tried to deflect the shot past Billy, but Billy got a pad on it and kicked it back to the corner. The winger beat Garry to the puck and dished it off to the defence, who began skating back and forth, trying to keep the play alive.

"One minute."

The defenseman fired a pass deep into the left corner. Samantha moved in to tie up her check, the two players battling with their skates and sticks for control of the puck. A second Bullets player moved in with his stick, trying to pry the puck free.

"Thirty seconds."

Sheldon left his check to support Samantha in the corner. Using up the last of his strength, he powered into the fray, shoved a Bullets player aside with his rear end and hooked the puck toward himself. He took one look up to scan the ice and skated behind the net. He knew exactly what he wanted to do.

"Cody!" he yelled. "Go!"

Cody had moved up high to cover the defenseman left alone when Sheldon moved into the corner. On Sheldon's cue, he skated to centre ice and took off.

Sheldon was just about to let the pass loose, when he was tripped by a stick thrust between his skates. He felt himself start to fall but refused to give up. Just as it seemed he was about to cough up the puck, Sheldon hooked it on his stick and rifled it straight up the middle, hitting Cody in stride just past centre ice.

"Ten seconds."

Cody didn't think about what he was doing or what this breakaway meant. He wasn't Sidney Crosby. He wasn't Bobby Orr or Doug Prefontaine. He was Cody Gladue.

Cody was focused solely on the goal, looking for any openings behind the goaltender. There were none—the Peace River goalie was playing him perfectly.

I'll make my own space, Cody decided.

As he closed in on goal, Cody faked a forehand shot then pulled the puck to his backhand. The goalie, now familiar with that move, waited for Cody to make his move then started to slide over to cover the backhand shot.

"Three seconds."

But the shot never came. As the goalie slid to cover the backhand, Cody pulled the puck back to his forehand. The goalie tried to scramble back into position, but it was too late. Cody let the puck fly with a snap of both wrists and watched his shot connect with the back of the cage. The referee arrived in a shower of ice, pointing at the net.

"Game over!" Chief Bullchild announced, but no one heard him. Every player, every parent, every spectator erupted in cheers as Cody raised his hands in the air.

The Warriors made their way toward him, throwing their gloves and helmets in their air before leaping on top of him. The weight was enormous, but Cody bore it with glee.

Final score: Warriors 4, Bullets 3.

As the players rolled off Cody, someone reached out and pulled him to his feet. It was Sheldon. His face clenched in pain, he wrapped Cody in an enormous bear hug.

Sandy was making her way onto the ice now, her eyes filled with tears. She traded hugs with her players then watched them line up and, in a tradition as old as the game, skate down the line of Peace River players and shake hands.

"What's the big deal?" a Bullets player asked Sheldon. "The game didn't mean anything."

Sheldon smiled. "This game meant more than you could ever understand," he said.

It was late, the Peace River Bullets long gone, but the players were only now starting to trickle home. The Warriors had gone into Manning for another organized-hockey tradition—pizza, purchased by the coaches—then returned to the rink to relive the game. It was dark, the night sky illuminated only by the waning moon.

The players were laughing and talking at the far end of the rink. Sandy and Doug were alone on the ice, holding hands and staring up at the sky.

"The stars don't look like this at home," Doug said, vapour trails spilling from his mouth.

"No, they don't," Sandy said. "Nothing does."

Doug turned to look at her, taking her hands in his.

"You want to stay, don't you?" It was more of a statement than a question.

Sandy nodded, a great sadness welling up inside her. "Yes," she managed. "I belong here. I have a purpose here. These kids have started something special. I want to help them build it."

Tears filled her eyes. She couldn't believe she was actually saying goodbye to the greatest love of her life. "The Bahamas are nice, but this is my home."

"Then it should be my home, too," Doug replied softly. He let go of one of Sandy's hands and dug into his jacket pocket.

"What?" Sandy asked, confused.

"Sandy Lafonde…" Doug began, lowering himself slowly onto one knee and producing a tiny box from his pocket.

Cody and Samantha were trading kisses underneath the bleachers.

"Cody, look!" Samantha whispered, pointing. They watched Sandy nod her head in an emphatic "yes" then wrap Doug in an enormous embrace.

"What happened?" Cody asked.

"They're getting married, silly!" Samantha said.

"Wow," Cody said. "That's cool."

"Cool? That's fantastic! Maybe we'll get to go to the wedding!"

Cody frowned. A thought had just occurred to him.

"Do you think that could be us someday?" he asked.

"We'll see," Samantha laughed. "If I have to wait that long, you had better be ready to fight a battle."

The moment had been a year and a half in the making, but that didn't make its arrival any less memorable.

The ribbon had been cut, the sweetgrass burned and the drums and dancers retired for the day. Now, every member of Watishka Lake First Nation was filing through the entrance of the Lawrence Arcand Memorial Arena.

The building wasn't huge by city standards, but it was the newest on the reserve. It encompassed a sheet of ice, team benches, four dressing rooms, a scoreboard and even a small Zamboni.

Doug Prefontaine had originally pitched the idea, not long after he and Sandy were married. He even offered up money from the sale of the house in the Bahamas to get it started. The band council and the provincial and federal governments chipped in the rest. The construction of the rink had generated jobs in the community and given some locals the chance to open up businesses, which meant even more jobs. The most important job—that of "rink rat," or facility manager—went to Doug, simply because he was willing to work for a very low salary.

The rink was located on the same spot as the original outdoor ice. As a result of the Warriors' performance against Peace River, the Manning Minor Hockey Association had offered to include teams from the reserve in its league, both boys and girls, at every age level.

It wasn't just a rink, though. Upstairs was a youth centre, where young people in the community could come and hang out any time. The newly appointed director of the youth centre was Sandy Prefontaine.

One of the most important guests had arrived the night before, even though he had to leave almost immediately. But Sheldon Lambert wouldn't miss this day for anything. He'd taken the bus from Peace River, where he was now playing

AAA midget hockey and turning some heads at higher levels, just to be home for the grand opening. The members of the Warriors team swarmed him when he arrived, trading stories about their big win one year ago.

Arm in arm, Doug and Sandy wandered outside into the cold, where Aunty Anne joined them. The reserve was quiet, as if finally at peace. The Posse had withered and died, the trailer park shut down.

"If I didn't know better, I'd say you planned all this," Sandy remarked to Aunty Anne.

"Just some of it dear," her aunt replied, giving Sandy a hug. "It was a team effort."

"How can it be a team effort if I didn't know what was going on?" Sandy asked.

Aunty Anne smiled. "That's not what I meant."

The old man watched from the tree line, as his granddaughter and great granddaughter chatted outside. A smile crossed his face. Both of them were beautiful. And both of them had taken action to save their community. Their work wasn't yet finished, but at least it had begun.

They had done well.

Turning back to the woods, the old man disappeared into the bush, leaving nothing but a whisper in his path.

ESCHIA
BOOKS

Here are more titles from
ESCHIA BOOKS...

TOM LONGBOAT
Running Against the Wind
by Will Cardinal
Tom Longboat was one of the greatest marathon runners of all time and one of the best known athletes of the western world in the early 20th century. Longboat was an Onondaga who grew up on the Six Nations reserve near Brantford, Ontario. He was an astonishing long-distance runner as an amateur, he set records as a professional and he served as a dispatch runner during World War I. This book tells the story of one of Canada's greatest athletes.
$14.95 • ISBN: 978-0-9810942-5-0 • 5.25" x 8.25" • 168 pages

VICTORIA CALLIHOO, BUFFALO HUNTER
An Amazing Life
by Cora Taylor
This is a biography of the woman who partly inspired Cora Taylor's beloved Our Canadian Girl character, Angelique. The celebrated children's book author recounts Victoria Belcourt Callihoo's story, growing up in an Alberta Métis community almost 150 years ago. Callihoo lived to be over 100 years old, seeing the Canadian West go from buffalo hunts and Red River carts to fast food outlets and cars.
$9.95 • ISBN: 978-0-9810942-4-3 • 5.25" x 8.25" • 192 pages

FIRST NATIONS HOCKEY PLAYERS
by Will Cardinal
This book features many First Nations hockey players who made it to the National Hockey League. Among them is Sandy Lake Cree member Fred Saskamoose of the Chicago Blackhawks, the first Native to play in the NHL. It also tells the stories of such players as Jonathan Cheechoo, Carey Price, Sheldon Souray, Jordin Tootoo, Bryan Trottier, Reggie Leach, Stan Jonathan, Theoren Fleury and Grant Fuhr.
$14.95 • ISBN: 978-0-9810942-1-2 • 5.25" x 8.25" • 176 pages